VampireVow

By *Michael Schiefelbein*

alyson books
los angeles | new york

MANUFACTURED IN THE UNITED STATES OF AMERICA.

THIS TRADE PAPERBACK ORIGINAL IS PUBLISHED BY ALYSON PUBLICATIONS,
P.O. BOX 4371, LOS ANGELES, CA 90078-4371.
DISTRIBUTION IN THE UNITED KINGDOM BY
TURNAROUND PUBLISHER SERVICES LTD.,
UNIT 3, OLYMPIA TRADING ESTATE, COBURG ROAD, WOOD GREEN,
LONDON N22 6TZ ENGLAND.

FIRST EDITION: JULY 2001

02 03 04 05 a 10 9 8 7 6 5 4 3

ISBN 1-55583-586-4

LIBRARY OF CONGRESS CATALOGING-IN-PUBLICATION DATA
SCHIEFELBEIN, MICHAEL.
  VAMPIRE VOW / BY MICHAEL SCHIEFELBEIN.—1ST ED.
  ISBN 1-55583-568-4
  1. VAMPIRES—FICTION. 2. GAY MEN—FICTION. I. TITLE.
PS3619.C36 V36 2001
813'.6—DC21   2001022575

COVER DESIGN BY MATT SAMS.
COVER PHOTOGRAPHY BY ROMA STUDIOS.

For Gary

I
Baptism Into Blood

One

I wanted Jesus. That's how it started. Yes, the Jesus they built a religion on, the one they say rose from the dead. (I should be the last creature in the world to doubt that.)

There we were, on a quiet, stony hilltop overlooking the city, the stars above us like light through pinpricks in black velvet. Just he and I, years before the 12 dolts who formed his entourage. We huddled next to each other as we often did, and I finally asked him.

"Joshu," I whispered—that was my name for him. "Why resist this? You're always talking about the vanity of human law, about wanting to strike out against the old order."

V

He looked troubled, a young man of 23 still as idealistic as his disgustingly naive, dull Nazarene parents, who actually believed me when I told them I was a Jew—I, a Roman officer serving under Pilate!

"I'm troubled," he said. He leaned back on his hands. The moonlight washed over his lean form, his fine brow betraying his sensuality as much as it did his intelligence.

"What's to be troubled about? Love? That's what you rant about all the time, isn't it? Love must replace the legalism of the priests." I stroked his cheek, the smooth cheek of an unmarried Jew boy.

He took my hand and kissed it. "You know what place you have in my heart. You are the earth itself to me. But the earth is passing—"

"This is pious trash." I jerked my hand away. "The truth is you lack the boldness to act by your beliefs. You're not a man of action. You're a poet brainwashed by the Essene fanatics walled up in their caves. All this business about the end of this age, the plight of the complacent priests. Then when it comes to a radical move—"

"You're talking about forbidden relations."

"Forbidden to whom?" I asked. I could hear him weakening, see him eyeing my strong calves, my bulky thighs. It was hot and I had thrown off my tunic to tempt him. Nature had given me a square jaw, a cleft chin, a dark mane, eyes that could bring a vestal virgin to her knees—and a cock that could keep her there. My meaty physique came from years spent in the Emperor's training rooms.

"The point is," I said, "we've sworn allegiance to each other. We meet on this craggy hillside night after night. I listen to all these dreams of yours about a kingdom of god. Your god. The stuff of sedition, I might add. We race along the river, buck-naked.

V

We even bathe each other! Ours is only the ultimate bond."

Right there, the Jew temple of Jerusalem beneath us, I swore to myself that I would finally enter him—the boy prophet, the ultimate challenge, my obsession. I would enter him the way I entered the Emperor's gates after a campaign: invincible, majestic. But hailed by his groans rather than by the cries of banner-waving masses.

I reached beneath his robe.

He pulled away. "No, Victor." His voice was not without regret. "I'm not ready to throw out the law of my fathers. This cannot happen."

This was the last time we met there.

Soon afterward I received a message from him: *I must give myself to no earthly man, only to my Father in heaven, for whose coming kingdom I must prepare. For the sake of this, we must meet no more.*

I persisted. I who had taken whomever I chose until that moment. I followed Joshu, hounded him until he fled to the desert to live as a hermit.

I had never hesitated to use force with other subjects of the Empire, to beat, to wrench them into submission. With this one, though, force could not be mustered.

Two

I met him a week after arriving in Palestine. After military training in Rome, my birthplace, and commanding troops in Gaul, I received a commission to serve in Judaea under Pilate, who'd replaced the puppet king, Archelaus, when he'd proved incompetent. My head swelled with the honor of it—living at Pilate's palatial headquarters on the Mediterranean coast, parading through the rabble of Jerusalem to remind the Jews whose empire they belonged to, spending the day wrestling naked soldiers and training in the governor's gymnasium. Besides quelling riots now and then and presiding over executions, all I had to do was bark orders and look good.

My hopes were crushed, however, as I and a fellow officer

V

surveyed Jerusalem for the first time from horseback. Beggars squatted at the city gates, pissed out in the open. The marketplace stank with overripe fruit and animal dung. Urchins ran naked through the streets, and toothless hags scrubbed linens at the wells.

Rome was not without its own squalor, but I had been exposed to little of it. I'd been raised outside the city in a magnificent villa with gardens, vineyards, and a superb view of the Apennines. The city drew me only after dark, when I needed a whore, when the lurid faces I passed in the night only excited my wild, drunken desires. In Rome, colossal buildings of marble overshadowed the ghettos. Fountains in enormous squares, mansions on the Palatine, the Circus Maximus, the baths of Caracalla, aristocrats draped in purple—the splendors of the city made up for its unpleasant corners.

While Jerusalem—aside from the temple (a shack by Roman standards), Herod's palace, and a few mansions—had nothing to offer but rank slums.

I got drunk every night the first week, depressed about being stationed in Judaea for three years. To hell with standards of Roman discipline, I thought. I needed an escape from that hole. After carousing one night after Pilate had left for councils in Rome, I shook off the clingy Egyptian whore who couldn't get enough of me and rode to the hills overlooking the city. A cool wind blew. The sky already burned pink on the eastern horizon. I dismounted, threw a blanket on a smooth rock, and passed out.

When I opened my eyes, the sun was setting. I'd spent a whole day sleeping off my stupor, but my head still pounded. A voice rose over a ridge just above me, a voice as smooth and sensuous as a wooden flute, a young man's voice. I scaled the rocks to peer over the ridge. A stark-naked boy, who seemed barely 20, cavorted on a bluff, throwing up his hands, swirling his head, all

V

the while chanting an eerie Oriental tune. His eyes were closed and I watched him freely for several minutes before he stopped directly in front of me and gazed down at the ledge where I stood, without a hint of shame in his handsome face.

"What's wrong, haven't you ever seen one before?"

He'd caught me admiring his dark circumcised cock, thick as a rope used to hoist building stones. "Not like that," I said. "You're my first naked Jew."

"It's a sign of the covenant," he said with pride, continuing to stand unabashedly in front of me with his arms crossed.

"Covenant?" His Latin was crude and I thought I'd misunderstood him.

"Yes, the covenant between us and our God."

"Demanding son-of-a bitch, if you ask me."

He sized me up as though he might kick me in the face, then laughed instead, his taut belly quivering. He laughed until he coughed and wiped tears from his almond-shaped eyes.

"Help me up, damn it. I'm tired of balancing on this ledge."

Still smiling, he offered me his hand, and I scrambled up to the bluff. He handed me a skin of water, exactly what I needed after a night of liquor and a full day of sleeping in the sun. Then we hiked to a lower level, leading my thirsty horse to a pool of water that had collected in a cave. He seemed to know every niche of the mountain, stepping with confidence in his dusty sandals across gullies and jagged stones. Still naked. In the twilight shadows at the mouth of the cave, his sinewy form and his long, unkempt hair seemed to belong to a wild man who roamed the mountains.

"Are you one of the crazy Essene cave dwellers I've heard about?"

"What makes you ask?" He stroked the neck of my horse as it lapped the water.

Michael Schiefelbein

V

"Don't tell me all Jews prance around on mountaintops with their peeled cocks flopping."

"No, just me."

"And why is that?"

"I'm strange, they say. I'm drawn to the mountains, up above Jerusalem. You can laugh, but I sense God here, even more than in the temple." He nodded in the direction of the city.

"Which god?"

"There's only one."

"Ah yes, a Jew idea. So you toss off your clothes when you feel the presence of your god?"

He smiled. "I go a little mad. Down there inside the temple walls, God seems confined. I know *I* feel confined."

"Watch out, Jew boy, you'll be stoned for heresy. I hear that's part of your religious code."

We secured my horse and climbed back to the summit where we'd met. It was too dark now to descend the mountain. We ate bread and lentils he'd brought in a pack, and stretched out on a homespun blanket to gaze at the lights in the city below. When the wind picked up, the boy slipped into his robe and lay close to me for warmth. He tantalized me more than any creature ever had, but I kept my hands to myself. Few, very few men could raise a sense of honor in me, but he—a Palestinian subject of the Empire, a Jew boy—managed somehow.

Over the next year, I became obsessed with him. We sailed on the Sea of Galilee, near his hometown, and hiked the rugged mountain terrain of Judaea. We feasted on roasted lamb, chugged his homemade wine until our vision blurred. Hot and drunk on the Mount of Olives, east of the city, we talked freely. He lampooned religious sects like the Pharisees and spun theories about the Elysian Fields, what he called the kingdom of Heaven.

In time he owned up to his heat for me—like I couldn't see it

V

in his eyes. It frightened him. But it wasn't fear that kept him from grabbing my balls. He had religious qualms. He was destined to be some kind of eunuch for his god, a damned vestal of Palestine.

His power over me never relented. Not when I inspected with contempt the modest stone house of his family in a neighborhood of Nazarene artisans, not when I watched him join dirty swarms of Jews outside the temple, not when I nearly exploded in unrequited lust.

If he'd toyed with me, if he'd held me at bay to stir up my desire, I'd have taken him in an instant. But he didn't tease. Nor did he fear me. He wanted me but wouldn't succumb. And I wanted nothing less than his will.

Our last night together, I was horny as a satyr and thought, *To hell with it, I've been a Stoic long enough—and when he feels my cock inside him he'll forget his scruples.* When he refused me, and cut me off, my rage knew no bounds.

Michael Schiefelbein

Three

"I'm sick of hearing of it, Lieutenant," Pilate said. He was flat on his stomach on his massage table, naked and glistening with oil. The man working his shoulder muscles was a barrel-chested Egyptian with braided black hair. The bath chamber was heavy with columns, gilded tiles, draperies. "It was one thing to beat the tax collector for cheating us above the usual amounts: He was an example. The defiant drunkard, too. But a woman with her baby? By the gods, man, we'll have a mob on our hands. We've got enough trouble the way it is."

These words from a man who loved bearbaiting.

"She was a prostitute, Your Excellency." I stood at attention above his bald head, my crotch level with his eyes. (I'd heard he

V

liked to carry on with his soldiers, though he'd never summoned me to his chamber.) "The people might have stoned her tomorrow for all we know, and she refused to obey my commands."

The governor signaled for the Egyptian to stop. The servant did so and brought him a sheet. Pilate wrapped himself in it and strolled to his couch. He stretched out on his side, eyeing the insignia on my tunic. His dark eyes were bold and cunning.

"She did not realize your rank, your position here?"

"Of course the bitch knew."

"And what did you command her to do?" He didn't bother trying to hide his curiosity.

"The usual things. I wanted to enter her backside. I wanted her tongue inside me. I wanted to bind her."

"And she resisted?"

"She tried. I tied her down, forced myself into her, with the brat looking on, bawling in his own shit. I backhanded him."

"Yes, well you might have spared the child." He motioned to a ewer of wine on a table and the Egyptian brought him a cup. "The Jews won't tolerate beating one of their children, even one that belongs to a prostitute. I've met with two contingents of their priests today."

"I'll restrain myself, Your Excellency."

"If you're hungry for blood, I can make you head executioner, Lieutenant." He eyed me impatiently over his cup.

"I will restrain myself."

"See to it that you do. I won't have another riot outside my walls." He waved me away.

In my dark room in the barracks, I removed my uniform and sandals and stretched out on my cot. The arched window framed a moon round and white as a discus. I knew I had gone too far. But since Joshu had dismissed me, fury had driven me to madness. What Pilate didn't know was that I'd knocked around

Michael Schiefelbein

V

other whores, as well as two or three Jew boys who'd tried to guard their circumcised shafts the way witless maidens guard their own treasures.

I had never wanted anyone like I wanted Joshu, a superior specimen of manhood—not just in his taut, athletic physique, but also in his thinking. He challenged not only the inane Jewish laws of ritual purity but, at least in private, elements of Roman civilization—the Emperor's title of divinity, social classes, the possession of slaves.

I shared his disdain. The difference between us was that I at least pretended to abide by the rules and obey the commands of my superiors. Such adherence had won me my rank, and I believed I was destined for greater things, perhaps direct service under Tiberius himself.

Now, however, my ruthlessness had spiraled out of control. My downfall was imminent if I could not restrain my animal urges.

Four

Other officers had sworn by the tranquilizing potions of a seer named Tiresia. I'd resisted entering the cluttered slum along one of the city walls where she kept shop, but now I was desperate for an elixir that would temper my anger.

Made of stone blocks, all of its windows bricked up, the former inn was entered through a small portal leading to a long, cavernlike corridor built against the wall. I stumbled in the darkness past three or four cubicles toward a dull light. I found the wench staring into a mirror of polished metal, oil lamps glowing around her. She saw my reflection and smiled triumphantly.

"So, you've finally come, Lieutenant Victor Decimus. Welcome to my lair. Sit here." She patted a stool next to her. She

V

wasn't the ancient hag I'd expected. She was not yet 40, her Ethiopian locks threaded with colored beads, her abundant bosom jiggling beneath her flowing robe with every movement she made.

"What, has another officer told you of me? Speak the truth, wench." I continued watching her in the mirror.

"The truth!" She laughed from deep in her chest. "I know nothing else. Nothing. If you please, my lieutenant, advance."

I approached the stool, removed my sword, and sat next to her.

"You're a handsome man, Lieutenant. You've a strong jaw, strong shoulders. Your eyes…they're bold, keen. You're a model client."

"I know what I look like. Enough of this prattle." I turned to her, but she averted her face from me.

"Please, my lord. Keep your eyes to the glass. If you want to be satisfied. Look only to the glass."

"If this is a game, I'll rip you apart, woman." I motioned to my sword and took a seat.

"You won't be sorry, my lord." Through the mirror, her heavy-lidded eyes again peered at me. She was a stunning beauty. "The remedy you seek, I have. I have something more, if you dare try it. However, it will stir up your passion rather than calm it."

"You must be a second-rate sorceress. The last thing I need is more of a temper."

"Ah, but what if you could be transported beyond the grounds of Pilate's headquarters? What if you could take whomever you pleased with no ill consequences?"

"Stop talking in riddles." I grabbed her arm, and she snapped her face away away from me.

"I promise, Lieutenant, I would not resort to tricks. What I offer is too grave for games. But you must not look at me."

"Why? I doubt you're afraid of a man's eyes, from the looks

V

of you. Why do you hide from the sunlight? Why is the shop as dark as a prison? Why do you cower here like a rat?"

"You must trust me, my Lord. There is no other way." She continued to face the darkness.

"Proceed." I released her arm and turned back to the mirror.

Without loss of poise she resumed her attitude before the glass. "What I have for you, you shall receive with no small pleasure. But again, you must trust me. I've waited long for you. I have seen you coming for an eternity. You're the first in an age. Without you I would shrivel and die. Stop!" She raised her hand when she perceived my impatience. Rings of rubies and polished jade glistened on her fingers. "You will understand soon enough. First, drink this." She reached for a silver ewer on a table and poured from it into a cup, which she handed me.

I sniffed it.

"There is nothing magical about it," she said. "It's merely a strong liquor to relax your resistance to my words. I speak the truth. Drink."

I did as she bid and very soon breathed more easily. The flame of a lamp transfixed me and I felt as though I lay in the sun after a swimming race in the sea. She slipped off her robe to show me her black breasts, round and full as silky pouches of spring water, waiting to be tasted by a parched desert nomad. Then she stood and let her garment drop to the floor. Her ebony body gleamed. Her ringed fingers touched my cheeks, guided me to her belly, which smelled of musk and sweet oil.

"Ah, this is all, wench? You want me to hump you?" I pulled her to the dirt floor. She moaned when my swollen cock sank into her warm, moist cunt. She moaned more as I pumped her, first slow, then hard, then slow to heighten my pleasure. All the while she kept her face turned from me.

The ride affected me like the opium I'd once taken in Rome,

V

producing a trancelike calm together with a keen, excited euphoria spreading from my loins through my body the way the heat of liquor in the stomach finally flushes the face.

She guided my mouth to her breast. My heart pounded as the brown nipple stiffened. At first I imagined that milk flowed from the breast, then I tasted something else, something warm and potent, something as rich and red as the wine of Capri, as exhilarating as a slash made by an opponent's dagger. When the liquid streamed down my chin, when I saw the stained breasts of the seer, I swallowed greedily. There was no stopping. The euphoria mounted.

I felt myself soar over the walls of the city on a moonlit night, over wells and courtyards, over crumbling stone dwellings wedged together on filthy streets. Below, lithe girls beckoned to me. Fair boys called for me to mount them. Amid them stood Joshu.

"So you see me, Victor!" he called from a rooftop garden. "You've discovered the power. But I promise, it will only trap you on the wrong side of eternity."

I soared round the roof, tried to light on its tiles, but could not descend. I was like a granule of chaff battling a whirlwind, while the palms below remained immobile in the silvered moonlight.

"You can't approach me, Victor. Believe me. Turn from her!" Joshu was as clear and distinct as a crow on white sand. None of the haziness of dreams obscured him, and I felt no awareness— as we often do in dreams—that what I saw would vanish if I willed myself awake. I was there, with him.

"Don't believe him, my lord." The seer's words burst into my mind, but I saw nothing of her as I soared, though the sensation of our coupling continued and I continued to taste blood in my mouth. "I am the way," she said. "Remember that. I am the truth."

"She mocks me. She mocks God," Joshu called.

"I will have you," I said. "I feel it. I feel it."

V

"You feel her."

"Enough for now, my lord." She pushed my lips from her breast. "More later if you like."

I was drenched with sweat, while she remained dry. The stain had disappeared from her breasts. I rolled off her to catch my breath.

"There's more, my lord. Why worry about your rage? You can find him whenever you like. And you can have much more besides. Much more." She propped her head on her elbow. In the shadows she had no need to turn her face away.

"What do you mean?"

"Come here again when you are ready to die."

"Are you raving mad, sorceress bitch?" I reached over and grabbed her throat. "I could strangle you now and leave you in this pit."

Suddenly a vise seemed to crush my hand, though I saw no culprit. I cried out in pain and tried, to no avail, to release myself.

"Remember what I've said, Lieutenant. I am the way. When you are willing to leave the world of the living I will take you to a place where you can be master of all. Even him."

My hand was freed from the invisible grip. Tiresia stood and, without moving toward her garments, was clothed.

"I want to see him again." I lay on the cold dirt, nursing my hand.

"You will not return here until you are prepared to stay."

She seated herself once again before the mirror and watched me stand and grope my way back through the dark corridor.

Michael Schiefelbein

Five

For weeks I could not escape the vision of Joshu on the rooftop, the sweet, powerful sensation I'd felt. I became convinced that had I remained with him longer I could have reached him, embraced him. And that locked in my arms, he could not have resisted me. I wrestled with the officers in Pilate's game hall, I drank myself to oblivion, I worked the whores and the boys who attended me. At night I paced the labyrinth of Jerusalem's narrow streets. Nothing relieved the restlessness.

I approached Tiresia's shop several times, once intending to feign agreement with her demands, but always the force I had felt on my hand returned, causing me to wince and massage my fingers. Unable to shake the invisible grip, I retreated.

V

My temper flared again and again. When my secretary misplaced a scroll, I beat him until he wept. When I found my chamber pot unemptied after breakfast, I shoved my servant's face in it. I raised my sword to a harlot when I found bloody discharge draining from her slit and made her beg for her life before I retreated from her house.

As long as I vented my rage on servants and whores, I stayed in Pilate's graces. But my restlessness reached feverish heights, and finally, delirium obliterated good sense.

The boy was a Jew. I had spotted him during a military parade near Herod's palace. Long-limbed, like a gazelle, he sunned himself on a wall, captivated by the glinting silver and plumage of our uniforms.

"You called me, sir?" He had come to my chamber, brought by the soldier I'd sent to retrieve him.

"Approach me, boy." I lay on my couch, surveying his soft features framed by black ringlets. "Closer. That's right." I fondled his woolen cloak. "What are you called?"

"Benjamin, sir." He stared straight ahead, out the window, not daring to drop his eyes to mine.

"Take off your cloak."

"Sir?"

"It's warm enough in here with the fire. Remove your cloak. There, that's better."

He was lean but solid. His neck rose like a delicate pedestal from his robe.

"Are you breaking some religious edict by being here? Never mind. You shouldn't worry your conscience. You had no choice. If you hadn't come… Do you have a family of some kind?"

"Sir?" He suddenly looked anxious.

"Oh, come now. I'm only asking from interest. I won't butcher them." I caressed his arm. My sense of protectiveness excited me.

V

"I have a mother, sir. A widow. She spends most of the day in prayer in the temple courts."

"Some kind of holy woman, I suppose."

"Yes, sir."

"Who looks after you? You can't be more than 14."

"I stay with my father's people, sir. They are potters."

"Ah, you've got good hands for that trade." I turned his hands over and examined the palms. "Sit here on my couch."

"Please, sir. I couldn't."

"But I command it." I pulled him to me. "Do you know what I want you for?"

"Do you want pottery, sir?"

"Look at me. Look at me, damn you!"

He looked at me as though I were going to recircumcise him.

"Do I look like I want pottery?"

"I don't know, sir."

Once he did know, he submitted like a lamb, stupidly following my directions without a sign of struggle. To break a boy in, to rob him of what most Jewish men never imagine surrendering, invigorated me more than a winter swim. When I was satisfied, I told him to dress and summoned my man.

"You'll breathe a word of this to no one, boy. For your family's sake. I warn you."

"Yes, sir." The boy stared blankly at me, as though stunned by days of exposure in the Judaean desert.

"Escort him to the gate," I said to my man, who had learned discretion from me the hard way.

The boy kept his word well. When his cousins tried to pry information from him, he kept silent. He lost his appetite, grew thin, stopped sleeping, ruined the pitchers and vases he was creating, burnt himself on the kiln. Then one day his cousin found him dangling from a tree, like an old woman's rug thrown

V

up to dry. He'd hanged himself after his mother, the wise bitch of a prophetess, guessed his shameful secret.

A delegation from the Sanhedrin stood before Pilate the next day. The results, I knew, would be imprisonment for me in Pilate's clammy cells, reserved for debauched or inept officers, followed by demotion, which would mean marching with the foot soldiers during military parades—to the satisfaction of the slimy priests on the sidelines.

Unbearable? Not for some. But I knew punishment like that would ignite my fury. Like the baited cheetah in the Roman circus, I'd tear apart my tormentors, dooming myself to longer imprisonment.

I fled the palace before Pilate could send his guards for me.

Six

In the whorehouse where I hid, incense burned night and day to camouflage the piss splattered in the corridors and courtyard by drunk patrons. The women painted their faces at night and floated up and down the halls in transparent silks, like ghosts, ghosts who returned to their grave beds by day. Not that customers did not demand service in the hours of sunlight—even pious Jews felt safe, knowing none of their kind ever showed his face in a neighborhood that would leave him ritually unclean. Then a ghost would be summoned from her grave by the shriveled mistress and display herself at the door, pale and naked, her eyes glassy and ringed by shadow.

The life of the night suited me to a degree. Hooded and

V

cloaked, I wandered freely through the black city and returned each dawn to pleasures of a new whore. But I was an officer, accustomed to showing off my physique, my badges, accustomed to dramatic displays of homage from miserable peons, accustomed to taking what I liked. My agitation became unbearable, as though I were subjected to a shrill, incessant flute. I considered escaping to Egypt or stowing away on a boat to Rome. But now I was a wanted man. News would reach Egypt and Rome before I was halfway to either place. In hiding or on the run, I could never live the life I deserved.

My thoughts wandered often to Tiresia's proposal. One night, after working a whore to a sweat, I interrogated her about the seer.

"I know nothing about her, sir. She's not one of us. We know all the competition." The girl was 16 at most, but already possessed of the jaded, weary expression that marked all whores. She sat on the floor, her head resting in her arms on the foot of the cot, after performing her finale. Candlelight flickered on her alabaster back.

"Don't tell me you've never seen the woman. Ethiopian or something. Black as the bottom of a cooking pot. She lives less than half a league from here." I lay naked on the cot, my hands behind my head.

"I swear, sir."

"What about the others? Surely they've seen her. Talked of her."

"It's possible, but they tell me nothing. I'm too new to be included."

"Yes. I'll bet they make piles of denarii on you." I touched her cheek with the ball of my foot. "I want you to talk to them at any rate. Get the information from your mistress. Tell her there's money in it for her."

"Yes, sir." The girl said it as though approaching her mistress meant abuse for her, regardless of profit to the proprietress.

Michael Schiefelbein

V

The next night, I got an answer I hadn't counted on—a contingent of Pilate's crew bearing shackles for me. Incensed at my inquiries about what she believed must have been a rival brothel, the mistress had arranged for my arrest. Fortunately the girl whore had taken a perverted liking to me. She flung open my door just after midnight.

"They're coming for you. Run, sir." Her chest heaved. Horror widened her normally listless eyes. She disappeared across the courtyard, a whirl of white.

Grabbing my tunic and a sack of gear, I climbed out the window and hurdled a low gate. Drawn by a force as strong as lust, I sprinted through alleys and back streets to the seer's house. This time I met no resistance to my entry.

"Welcome, Lieutenant." Tiresia sat enthroned in her place before the mirror, her reflection glimmering softly in lamplight.

"Who are you?" I demanded, panting at the doorway of the shadowy chamber.

Tiresia laughed and stroked the colored beads in her hair. "Oh, Lieutenant. Your nature will serve you well on this side of the night."

"Face me!" I flung down my bag and approached her, but thought better of clutching her after the hand-crushing I'd received before.

"You are prepared now to join the league of the night? You've destroyed hopes for success in a mortal life."

"I'm here to hide, wench, and nothing more." I sank onto a bench and wiped the sweat from my brow. A rat scurried along the wall and vanished behind broken furniture and piles of rags.

She raised her head and studied me from beneath her heavy eyelids. "When you emerge from this house, Lieutenant, you will never hide again. You've only tasted what I can give you. Wait until you feel the full pleasure of complete power over mortals,

V

the ability to travel, to soar over continents at the speed of thought. Wait until you can crush whom you please with impunity, command anyone you will."

"What about him? The one I have wanted to taste as I have wanted no other."

"Why do you want him?" She seemed displeased.

"Why? If you know so much, you must know why."

"I know all about him. But do you?"

"More riddles." Impatient, I rose and peered down the corridor. Then I turned to her. "He's told me I'll never approach him. He's told me you lie."

"Of course. He wishes to keep you away."

"But I desire him. I want him as my beloved. And he desires me in return. I know it."

"Exactly, my dear Lieutenant. He sees you as a test of his faith."

"Damn this god he imagines. A moment with me will turn him into an apostate."

Tiresia smiled. She dropped the robe from her raven shoulders. Her breasts, nipples purple in the lamplight, rose and fell as she breathed, like floats on a calm sea. "Come to me."

Heated by her charms, I stripped, spread my cloak over the cold earthen floor for her to lie on, and mounted her. Once again she turned her face to the shadows.

"Why me?" I asked in the midst of her moans. "Why not the others, the officers who've come for your potions?"

"Oh, my lieutenant." She clutched my buttocks to drive me more deeply into her. "There were no others. The words…were planted in their minds." Groaning with delight, she guided my lips to her breast. "Drink, my Victor. Drink."

The warm blood oozed from her nipple. The sight of it maddened me. I lapped it up like a starving dog. I sucked long and hard, until my whole body became as engorged with blood

V

as my cock. The sensation I'd felt before returned, the strange sense of euphoria mixed with acute vision and heightened power. I could have strangled a bull with my bare hands.

"Yes, Victor. Keep drinking. You mustn't stop this time."

I had pulled away from her to get my breath, as though we'd been locked in a kiss of passion. She pulled me back to the wet teat.

"Drink and live."

Suddenly a pain shot through my skull and then concentrated in my eyes. They pounded. I thought they would explode in my head. But despite the torture, I clung to Tiresia's supple body. My loins continued to hammer against hers at a furious pace. Then, like a fountain, the seer's breast poured forth liquid that was no longer hot and salty, but cool and refreshing—blood still, but a chilled elixir that somehow dulled my pain.

My sense of strength redoubled. I felt like a man charged with superhuman energy in a time of disaster, mighty enough to lift a block of granite from a worker crushed beneath it. I soared as I had soared in our last encounter, above the tiled roofs, the palms and walls of Jerusalem. Higher and higher. Through clouds. Toward a sliver of moon. Toward blackness—not empty, but full of creatures, heads and hands and limbs. The beings peered at me from behind treelike shadows.

"You are approaching it, Victor." Tiresia whispered into my ear. "Ah, yes. You're almost there."

But where? By the gods, where?

The sweat that had soaked me as our mad coupling began suddenly evaporated. My skin tingled, cool and taut. I was aware of every inch of my body and at the same time attuned to the darkness around me as I soared.

Tiresia laughed. "This is the beginning of time, Lieutenant. My time, my birth into the night. You are returning me here to reign. I have proven myself. It has taken centuries, since the time of the

V

great Sphinx, but it is finished. Now I join the court of darkness."

Lightning ripped through the night. I could see Tiresia distinctly next to me. Her garments fluttered in a whirlwind as she flew. Her beautiful face had become translucent. The beads in her hair shimmered like precious stones. Other figures, robed, crowned, surrounded her in the air. They caressed her face with long, tapered fingers. They deposited a crown upon her head and carried her away, fading into the blackness.

"Wait! Damn you, wait! What about me? What do I do?"

"Follow your instincts, Victor." Her cry rolled out in her wake. "Follow your instincts. You will know." The final word echoed through the dark vault, slowly fading.

Conscious of returning, in an instant, to Tiresia's shop, I rolled off her motionless, cold body. I lowered the oil lamp to examine her face. The shriveled features and sunken cheeks of a hag glowed in the light—the hideous face she had hidden from me. Before my eyes, her luscious breasts dried up and disintegrated.

That is how it began.

Michael Schiefelbein

Seven

Behind a false wall in Tiresia's chamber, I found her sarcophagus, lined with hieroglyphics chiseled in ancient Egypt. There I slept by day for the next eight years, at night glutting my thirst on the blood of beggars and rich merchants, boys and maidens. I even rampaged Pilate's household, first unnerving his pathetic wife, who rambled about visions of black ghosts in her room, then sinking my fangs into the breasts of his best servant girls, their juice exploding in my mouth like plump fruit.

My cock swelled as I drank blood, and the sensation—the heat, the lusty ecstasy—transcended any erotic pleasure I'd ever had.

It didn't take long, however, for me to tire of satiating my thirst, of testing my new strength, of flight, and of preternatural

V

vision. I, like all beings, craved company. But I existed in isolation. I knew others like me existed, but not in Jerusalem. We were assigned domains by the dark powers, and our provinces did not overlap. Strange voices told me this in dreams.

Whores and boys of the street entertained me at night, and vagabonds cast dice with me. I paid my debts to them with silver piled up in Tiresia's secret chamber, from what source I knew not.

But there was only one man I wanted.

After a month of refining my powers, I found Joshu bathing in the river after dusk. From behind the reeds, I watched his sinewy arms stretch as he scrubbed his back. I inspected his thighs, as strong as columns, his belly, taut as a drum. Light lingering on the horizon painted his angular features and left the shadow of his form on the shallow water.

"Who's there?" He scanned the shore as I rustled through the reeds.

"It is I, Joshu." I stepped into a clearing on the bank.

"I thought you were dead. Where have you been?"

For the first time the aura of strength about him, spiritual strength expressed in every firm muscle of his body, struck me as superhuman. For the first time a strange shudder of apprehension passed through me.

"Who are you, Joshu?"

"I have told you, Victor. I am my father's son."

I splashed through the water toward him. I stopped so close to him I could see the tiny scar on his temple that he'd told me about. A neighbor boy had struck him with a rock when he was six or seven. "Which god is your father?"

"I have told you. The only god." He stooped over and cupped his hands to drink.

I clutched his arm. "The Roman gods are much more powerful than this god of the Jews. They outnumber him after all."

V

"What have they done for you?" He straightened and faced me boldly. In the light of the rising moon, his eyes revealed his love for me.

"They've made me immortal."

"Have they?"

"It's what you always speak of, isn't it? An eternal realm. Well, I've found it."

He quietly contemplated my face.

I pressed my lips against his and for a moment he leaned toward me, but then drew back.

I snorted at his rebuff. "I thought you told me I could not approach you."

"When did I tell you that?"

"In the vision.

"I don't know of what you speak."

"Deny it if you like. But here's the truth. I've the power to take you. But why should I, Joshu, when you want me? Be my consort. I can grant you immortality."

"You can never possess me." Joshu started toward the shore.

I grabbed his arm and pulled his naked body to me. "I already possess you." I shoved him away and, with a flicker, sped through the night, as light and invisible as the wind.

Wherever he went, I hounded him. When he retreated to the desert like one of the crazy Essenes, I squatted next to his campfire. When he paced the temple courts beneath the starry sky, I blocked his path. When he slept at the homes of those who had begun to follow him, I boldly marched through their doors.

"Why are you doing this?" he screamed one night in the desert, where he'd gone to pray. I sensed I had not been the only devil to tempt him there in the darkness. "What do you want?"

"You know what I want." I stretched out on the blanket he had spread before the fire.

V

"Robbing my purity means that much to you? What if you did take my body? My soul would belong only to my Father." He looked weak and drawn in the rippling light.

"Save that pig fodder for the masses, Joshu. Piety means nothing to me. And as far as you're concerned—you want me too. I'll wage war on you until you weaken, my friend. You're body isn't enough for me. I can have any I choose. I want your soul."

He suddenly broke into a fit of laughter. "Oh, Victor, had you wanted my love, my company, my teaching…. But my soul?"

"Do you know who I am?" I sat up and glared at him.

"I know you belong to the night with the other demons. Except…"

"Except what?"

"For you there's still hope."

"Damn you!" I leaped up, ripped off his cloak, and threw him to the sand. I pinned back his arms and spread his legs with my knees. "Is there hope now?"

I tore at his throat with my fangs, but the second I tasted his blood a wave of nausea passed through me. I vomited the blood from my earlier victims into the sand.

"Who is protecting you? Who is keeping you from me?"

"I am free. No one commands my will. Not even my God. But I have surrendered to him." He sat up and rubbed his arms where I had gripped him. Then he reached for his cloak.

"They say you work miracles. Why don't you cast me away from you as you cast away the demons from the godforsaken creatures roaming the slums?"

His response was a prolonged gaze at me, as though he were actually considering using his powers. But his gaze also held compassion.

"You're a holy fool," I said, spitting out a remnant of the blood that had erupted from my throat. "You'll never rid yourself of me."

V

Indeed, I kept after him, hounding him until the very end of his divine crusade, when even his charisma couldn't save him. In the final days I nearly had him. Immortality in my company looked pretty good to someone condemned to die.

On the day when the sky darkened to the shade of midnight, I rose from my tomb and soared to Golgotha. Gazing lustfully at Joshu from the foot of his execution cross, fighting my urge to lap up the blood that dripped from his hands and feet, I invited him one last time. He listened to me but merely turned his eyes to the sky, invoked his god, and slipped into a death I will never know.

For two nights I ransacked Jerusalem's streets, torturing, murdering whoever came into my path, mangling limbs and tearing flesh with my teeth, without stopping to suck out the elixir after my first few victims.

Then, just before dawn that Sunday, as I hurried back to my refuge, it happened. I felt him.

"Joshu! What is this? What kind of spirit are you?"

I glanced around the street, gray in the harbinger glow of morning. "Show yourself to me."

He stood before me, naked and whole, not pale from death. The nail marks still on his feet and hands looked more like small tattoos than wounds.

"I am not a ghost, Victor. I live."

"As do I, my beloved." I stepped toward him, but the dawn was moments away and I had to flee. "Come with me, to safety."

But he stood immobile and I could not hesitate another second.

When I awoke later in the darkness, I felt as though I were the only being left on an annihilated earth. Joshu was gone from me. I knew this before his followers began babbling about a resurrection. He existed, was immortal, but not in a world of darkness like mine. I howled like a wolf who'd devastated a flock of sheep and was now left with nothing. It was only then that I

V

believed in the god Joshu returned to, a god of light. And it was then that I vowed to avenge my loss on this pompous being who had deprived me of the only one I ever loved.

II
The Cloister

Eight

"Abbot Reginald of St. Sylvester speaks well of you, Brother Victor. He says you have much to offer us here at St. Thomas." Brother Matthew, a burly man, stood before a tall window in his office. He was abbot of St. Thomas, my new home, but he told me he didn't like titles. "Brother" suited him just fine.

The window looked out into the courtyard, where a gnarled old pine basked in the light of a full moon. The walls of the office bulged with thick, musty volumes. The oak floor and desk were blackened with age.

"I'm grateful for the abbot's recommendation, Brother Matthew." I assumed the tone of deference I'd perfected through centuries of monastery-hopping. Also robed in black, I sat

V

across from him in a leather chair, venous with cracks.

"We Thomists have never accepted a monk from another order. But the accident was tragic—the demise of an ancient community stemming from the Dominicans, like ours. Order of the Divine Word—splendid name. What a pity." He shook his head.

"Yes." I studied the fat neck that rose from his black habit. His ripe jugular bulged as big as the infant snakes we ate as delicacies in Pilate's headquarters two millennia before.

"The fire was sudden?"

I nodded. "It was a medieval abbey, full of rotting wood. England is full of decrepit abbeys and convents. The unusually strong winds on the English heath didn't help. When the fire started, everyone was asleep. They weren't due to rise for matins for another hour. And the fieldwork had been grueling that day, especially for the older monks. Most everyone died of smoke inhalation. Through God's mercy I was taking my usual walk on the heath, safe from the sun's rays. My skin condition won't cause inconvenience, will it?"

"Of course not, Brother Victor." The abbot seated himself in the leather chair behind his desk. The lamp cast a rosy glow on his smooth cheeks. His eyes were small and closely set and full of the disgusting charity I never grew tired of loathing. "It's a strange condition, I admit. What a misfortune to be intolerant of the sun. Though the night has its own beauty."

"Indeed."

"And you can work in the night? It will be good to have a sentinel of sorts."

"The underground cell is not a problem?"

"Not if you don't mind the damp rooms beneath the chapel. It's where we said our private masses in the old days—a network of dank little chapels and storage rooms. We've furnished a cell for you down there. I promise you you'll not see a single ray of sun."

V

"Excellent. The crypt is around there too, I suppose? The one you mentioned to Abbot Reginald?"

"Yes. I hope that won't bother you—sleeping among our faithfully departed. They're good old souls." He smiled benevolently.

"Indeed not. I can pray better in that environment, reminded of mortality." I mustered a smile, and he, predictably, reciprocated. "I have a trunk full of books. They're out in the car."

"I'll get a brother to help you." Brother Matthew picked up the phone. "I'm surprised Brother Cyril didn't bring it in already."

"That's my fault. I told him I'd get the porter to help me after I spoke to you. He did carry my other bags to my cell."

The abbot shifted the receiver and gave directions to the porter I'd glimpsed as old Brother Cyril had pulled into the parking lot, a willowy boy of 19 or 20 who blushed when I saw him peering out the window.

I rose when he knocked at the door and the abbot called for him to enter. He was indeed a specimen—full lips, limpid eyes, a shock of blond hair, the bangs curling over his eyebrows. He smiled bashfully at me, then turned his attention to the abbot to receive his instructions.

"Brother Victor," Brother Matthew called as we were leaving. "Why exactly did Abbot Reginald survive the fire? He wasn't clear in his letter or phone call."

"I think he was out of the building too, Brother. He suffered from insomnia."

"I see. And he really won't accept our hospitality?" The abbot squinted in the lamplight.

"He's very old. His community is gone. He wants to be with his family in Brighton." I tried to restrain my impatience at his irritating concern.

"I see. Welcome to America, Brother, and to the monastery of St. Thomas. We'll try to help you not miss England too much.

V

Make yourself at home."

"Yes, Brother. Thank you."

How many times over the ages had I introduced myself to an unsuspecting abbot? It was in the late 13th century that I entered the first cloister, a Dominican fortress in the Apennines full of boys hardly old enough to shoot their loads. That's when I set out in earnest on a calculated campaign to destroy the harems of Joshu's god. I'd only begun to hear about monasteries, although apparently the communities of monks had spread from Egypt into Italy 200 years before.

But let me start at the beginning.

After the death of Joshu, I spent a dozen frustrating years waiting, searching for his spirit among the old Palestine haunts. Then, despondent, I made my way back to Rome, where I spent four centuries feasting on the rich blood of patricians and the exotic blood of slaves from every corner of the empire. The Germanic invasions began in the fifth century. At first I enjoyed the excitement, the chaos. I could smell blood from the battle-fields when I emerged from my hiding places after sunset. But depression gradually set in as I watched the collapse of civilization as I'd known it.

I left Rome in the eighth century and wandered through the Far East until the Barbarian raids were long over. Then I returned. More than a millennium had passed since I'd beheld Joshu. A millennium. I caught wind of these idealistic followers of Joshu huddled together, renouncing the world as he had. It seemed too good to be true. My nocturnal wanderings, glutting my appetites, had begun to bore me. I lacked a purpose, stable companionship, things I thought I could dispense with on the dark side of existence. The challenge of the secluded abbeys where pietistic young males wrestled with their carnal desires, where Joshu's spirit perhaps lingered, where I could most injure

V

his god...that challenge baptized me into a new life. The night once again held promise.

The first millennium after Joshu's death was my adolescence as a predator, my youthful heyday. In the second millennium, as a monk, I enjoyed the fruits of experience: more finesse in my dealings with humans; more restraint over my cravings; more single-mindedness in my hunts; more concentration, hence ecstasy, in my feedings.

Between the 13th and 20th centuries, two dozen monasteries, in Italy, France, Spain, Germany, and the British Isles, harbored a creature of the grave unknowingly—until too late. With each abbey I left devastated, I cut a new notch in the belt squeezing my heart, the belt strapped there by Joshu. If I couldn't remove it, I could gloat over its defacement.

St. Thomas would make two dozen and one notches. And my first in the New World.

Leaving the abbot's office, I followed the boy monk, Brother Luke, down the dark hallway into the medieval-looking foyer of St. Thomas Abbey. Our feet thudded on heavy oak planks. High above us loomed thick rustic beams. The abbot had instructed the young porter to give me a tour of the buildings.

"Would you like to see the chapel first?"

Though I wasn't an expert on American accents, his drawl seemed rural. He pointed toward heavy doors surmounted by a carved image of Joshu on the abominable crucifix, the one I had stood before 2,000 years ago. In all that time I had not grown immune to the longing and bitterness the image evoked.

"Lead on, O Gabriel." I squeezed his shoulder when he beamed at the name of the angelic guide.

Lights from votive candles flickered before statues in side altars and near the sanctuary of the long, narrow chapel—an unimaginative variation on chapels since the beginning of

V

monasticism. Choir stalls faced each other near the sanctuary, and pews lined the body of the church. The place smelled of incense and candle wax, old varnish and sickly-sweet flowers.

"You wanna offer a prayer?" The boy whispered as though the empty chapel were filled with meditating monks.

"Thank you. Please, come with me." I touched his back.

We walked side by side down the center aisle and knelt at the communion rail. The golden tabernacle doors were embossed with a predictable scene of the "last supper." The truth is, Joshu was sick during that final Passover and couldn't eat a thing. I teased him about it—and scoffed at the foot-washing ritual that embarrassed his foul-smelling men, their feet caked with filth. He had an irresistible penchant for degrading himself.

But he had enough sense to avoid ending up imprisoned in a bread box. The Blessed Sacrament indeed! And even if he was in the tabernacle, it wasn't as a wafer that I wanted to taste my Joshu.

Brother Luke amiably gabbed as he led me through the other buildings forming the sides of the large courtyard, thick with hedges and trees now dormant in the January cold: a high-vaulted library adjacent to the chapel was in one building; in another was a social hall, a kitchen, and a refectory with two long tables for the handful of monks who lived there; a third building contained a dormitory of tiny cells, administrative offices, and, adjacent to the foyer, a richly furnished parlor for receiving guests. A fairly new greenhouse had been constructed on the north side of the refectory, behind the buildings.

"There's a room of computers next to the library. But I ain't got the key." Boy Luke stood timidly behind a heavy chair. "They put in a lot of time in there, with their research and all."

"And you have no scholarly ambitions? I thought the Thomist order pledged to carry on the work of the great St. Thomas Aquinas." Through my research I had learned all about

V

the 19th-century offshoot of the Dominicans. Most of the monks were scholars who did research at the monastery during extended university sabbaticals. Between the monastery's enormous library collections and its modern computer technology, they had all the resources a pinheaded professor could want. They would keep their noses buried in their books and stay well out of my way.

"Gotta have porters and groundskeepers, too." He smiled sheepishly.

"Ah, I see. You are responsible for the charming landscaping, then?"

"Me and Brother Michael. We tend the greenhouse, too."

"And is Brother Michael a stooped old farmer?"

Luke shook his head. "He ain't but five years older than me. Lot smarter though. Reads like a fiend. Just not interested in scholar stuff."

As the boy helped me unload my trunk from the car, I surveyed the landscape in the moonlight: the long dirt path to the monastery snaked through trees and down a hillside until it hit a country road, invisible from the promontory. Behind the buildings, acres of woods rose to the Appalachian peaks that now looked like bites taken from indigo paper. We were far from the city of Knoxville, from heavy settlement, but I smelled human blood in the cold night air, as I'd known I would.

My stay here would be short if I fed on monks again. This time I would resist the urge even longer than I had the last time. Once I started on monks—sick of feeding on drifters and prostitutes and other refuse no one missed—once I started on monks I couldn't control my appetite for their consecrated flesh, which carried me to orgiastic heights. I would grow careless, leaving trails of blood, missing the suppers I only pretended to eat anyway, missing compline—unable to stomach invocations

V

of Joshu. In the bloody chaos, clues would point to me and I would have to flee once again, often destroying the monastery as I had recently done in England, when the good brothers of St. Sylvester discovered too much.

My cravings defeated my own purpose. I intended to steal the souls of devout boys, not their mortal lives. Controlling a boy thrilled me as terrifically as it had during my existence as a man. My cock still hardened. I could still take a boy, though it was the sight of him surrendering his will to me, not the friction of fucking, that triggered my orgasm.

I took no pleasure in barring the doors of St. Sylvester's, in torching the carpets and draperies, in razing the buildings that had given me security. But I had no choice, and no choice but to assume the identity of Abbot Reginald in order to make arrangements at St. Thomas. This time I would resist longer. I would stick to the indigenous food.

"People live in the mountains?" I asked, lugging one side of the trunk while Luke took the other.

"Some. Most is miners. But the mines done closed." Luke's breath steamed before him in the cold. "They get by on whatever they can shoot in the woods or pull out of the dirt. Michael takes them food and supplies."

"Indeed."

Inside the foyer, Luke unlocked a door that opened onto a dark and narrow stairway beneath the vestibule of the chapel. He flicked on the light and turned to take his side of the trunk.

"It'll be easier if I carry it myself." I picked up the trunk and he moved out of my way.

"My God, do you lift weights or something?"

I grinned, feeling his eyes admiring me from behind—for when I chose to I could feel any senses directed at me. "Natural, brute strength, my friend." He did not know the half of my powers.

V

Deep in the bowels of the church, we walked along a flag-stone corridor, past alcoves made of brick, like burial niches in the Roman catacombs where I fed upon the neophyte Christians: the first martyrs—because of me, not the lions. The widely spaced incandescent bulbs along the walls shined upon marble altars within the alcoves.

"The ordained brothers used to say their masses down here." Luke was leading the way now. "Don't see how you can sleep so close to the graves. Gives me the creeps."

"With the Blessed Sacrament just above me? How can I be afraid, Luke?"

"Still…"

"Ah, I see we're coming to the crypt." Engraved marble tablets spaced six feet apart lined the walls. Six names were engraved on each of the tablets, which were embedded in the wall above an iron door that was soldered shut. I'd seen this sort of mausoleum many times: the coffins inside the small chambers were sealed in vaults, stacked in pairs. "How long has it been since a brother died?"

"That'd be Brother Raymond, last year. Ninety-two years old. There he is." Luke pointed to one of the last mausoleums. The soldering was shiny still.

I deposited my trunk on the floor of my cell, a small storage room beyond the crypt, which had been furnished with a bed, a desk, shelves, and a chest of drawers. In a room across from mine, plumbing had been installed for the priests who said their masses near the crypt. A duct from the boiler room directed meager heat into the entire subterranean space.

It was after midnight, and I was growing ravenous, not having fed since the night before when I broke out of the coffin being shipped on a flight from London. When Luke offered me a fraternal embrace to welcome me, I wanted to pierce his supple throat and

V

drink. I clutched him as I clutch my prey, willing him to immobility. Within his stunned body, I felt him succumbing. In that second I could have ordered him to do anything, he was so pliable. Latent homosexuals—a category that obviously fit him—were always the easiest to control in monasteries, where such creatures flourish. But there was no hurry. Young Luke could wait. I released the boy and he pulled away, embarrassed but not sure why.

Minutes after he had ascended to his cell, I was once again in the night air. The scent of blood drifted through the dense woods. I tore through branches, over frozen soil and brittle leaves, my preternatural sight steering me though the darkness in the direction of my prey.

The wooden shack, its porch sagging and windows boarded, nestled into the mountainside near a frozen brook. A doorless old refrigerator and a heap of rusty cans and other garbage littered the ground beside it. Light bled through the windows. Inside, a baby cried. I stood on the porch, listening to a husky-voiced woman singing. Before she could finish her lullaby, I charged through the door.

The woman, seated on a kitchen chair, cradling the baby in her arms, screamed. Of course my appearance was horrible, as always when I fed. My skin took on the jaundiced hue of a new corpse. My fangs grew in an instant to the length some stalactites take a century to reach. Fire burned in my eyes. I panted like a rabid dog.

"Oh God, please. No!" She clutched her baby to her breast when I reached for it.

I snatched the brat from her, raised it to my mouth, and, shaking off the blanket, sank my teeth into its soft belly. Its blood squirted like the juice of a plump tomato in my mouth.

Shrieking hysterically, the woman grabbed at the baby, but I held it firmly, draining it and dropping the corpse on the dingy

V

linoleum floor. She scrambled from her chair and threw herself on her dead child. Snatching a handful of her oily hair, I pulled her to her feet and ripped off her sweatshirt. She reeked, as though she hadn't bathed in a month. Her face was pock-marked. But her breasts, swollen with milk, enticed me. My fangs sliced into them. Her eyes rolled back. Her head dropped and her body went limp. When I'd had my fill, I let her crumple to the floor beside her child.

I hauled their bodies to the heart of the dark woods and flung them into a ditch, rolling a fallen tree over them. Then I returned to the shack and wiped up stray drops of blood. Anyone searching for the victims in their remote dwelling—whoever supplied their food and fuel—would assume they'd vacated and trudged to the warmth of the city.

Shortly before dawn I raced back to my cell. Stuffing pillows under the blanket in case anyone should look in on me during the day, I left the cold cubicle and hurried to the crypt. The iron door of old Brother Raymond's mausoleum gave easily under my strength. I slipped into the dark, cramped chamber, where I had to stoop like a humpback, and pulled the gate firmly shut behind me. The lingering smell of decay, no longer detectable to a mortal, wafted to my nostrils, at once familiar and repugnant. Tracing the odor to the top vault of the third pair of tombs, the one farthest from the door, I pried it open. The plain pine cas-ket was perfectly intact, probably the only one in the whole crypt in such a condition. I opened the lid, scooped out the skeleton, still dressed in a habit, dumped it on the floor to be discarded later, and climbed into the coffin. Within seconds of closing the lid, I drifted off, sated and exhausted.

Nine

I did not need to feed every night. Sometimes I could last a week or more if I'd imbibed enough blood. The woman and her baby had glutted me. I went for 10 days before killing again, this time a tramp who lived in a hovel of corrugated metal. In the first month at St. Thomas I fed on several more mountain people, careful to bury their remains in the woods to avoid raising alarm.

After centuries of inhabiting monasteries, I slipped easily into a routine. Rising just after sunset, I joined the brothers at table because it was expected of me, even though I always arranged to eat my own meals in the kitchen at times appropriate for a nocturnal schedule to keep hidden my inability to take normal food. While they swallowed their stew, the 23 men—most in

V

their 50s and 60s with a few younger monks scattered about, all garbed in black, hooded robes—listened to readings from Thomas à Kempis's *Imitation of Christ* or from the works of their fat hero, Aquinas. (I'd never lived with that medieval scholar's community, but I had met many monks who confirmed rumors that a semicircle had been carved into the dining table to accommodate his piggish girth.)

After dinner came a period of recreation. The monks could gather in the social hall or exercise in the basement gymnasium. Compline was chanted at 8 in the dimly lit choir stalls. Then the monks filed to their wretched holes. Fortunately, the chanting of matins had long ago been abandoned by the group; being in my assigned stall at 3 in the morning used to take some maneuvering, especially when my victims took me far from the grounds. I usually attended compline, as much as I loathed it—hearing Joshu's name again and again, the words about his blood, his body, at once a mockery of my own feedings and a reminder that I could not possess him. I was always half afraid that I would storm up to the altar and rip open the priest's throat.

But of course I did no such thing.

Instead, very easily, I exerted ever-increasing control over young Luke. I had him violating the Grand Silence within a few weeks. He would sneak down to my cell after compline, eager as a spaniel who wanted petting. He sobbed to me more than once about the mother who abandoned him after the death of his father, about the stern grandfather who raised him.

"Very sad," I said after one of his crying jags. "Come sit by me." I patted the cot I'd never slept in.

He rose from the desk chair and settled on the bed, nestling against my shoulder. His wet cheeks gleamed in the light of the candles burning on the bookshelves. I detested the overhead fluorescent tubes.

V

"That's better, isn't it?"

He nodded. "Victor…." He paused.

"Why have qualms?" I could hear his thoughts, like the confused voices of children on a playground. "What could be better? God has brought us together."

"Do you think so?" He sniffed.

I dug a handkerchief from my pocket. "Here, blow your nose."

He did as I directed, then said, "Brother Matthew talks about particular friendships. The *Imitation* says they're the work of the devil."

"Has the good abbot spoken to you about us?"

He avoided my eyes. "No. In his sermons, I mean."

"What about the others?" I glared at him. "Do they talk of you and me?"

"Not really." He lowered his eyes once again.

"Tell me the truth."

"Well, Mike has asked a thing or two," he finally admitted, sheepishly.

"Brother Michael wanted information about me?"

"Not information, really. Sometimes when we're working in the greenhouse he asks things."

"What kinds of things?"

"Well, he asked about your order."

"And what did you tell him?" I stood and walked to the desk.

"Nothing. I don't really know nothing but what Brother Matthew told us all. You was in some other kind of Dominican order in England, Order of the Divine Word, and the monastery burned down and the other brothers died. And it was our duty to take you into our community. You never told me nothing else."

I leaned against the desk with my arms crossed, examining his childlike face. "Tell me, if Brother Michael's as intelligent as

Michael Schiefelbein

V

you say, why is he content to spend the day doing mindless work in a greenhouse?"

Luke twisted his mouth to one side and contemplated the question. "I expect it's a spiritual thing. He's damn holy. God comes first in everything. Maybe working the soil is good for his soul."

I pondered the crucifix above the bed. I'd left it there to avoid rousing suspicion. "Why didn't you tell me about Michael's curiosity?"

"I…I don't know. I never told him nothing, though. Not about breaking the Grand Silence or coming down here. I won't say nothing about you anymore."

"Never mind, Luke." I turned my eyes back on him. "Talk to him all you want about me. Now you'd better leave. It's nearly midnight."

Ten

From then on I paid special attention to young Brother Michael, whose good looks and intensity I'd already noticed during compline, when he sang the psalms with such fervor one would have thought he'd already entered the courts of paradise—or that he feared losing paradise altogether. I liked the latter possibility much better.

I'd seen many monks like Michael in my time: cocky, full of themselves, aware of their brawn and handsome features, of their intelligence and charisma. Yet at odds with themselves because of their strange ideas about religious perfection. Why in hell they did not stop resisting their gifts and make the most of them…well, I didn't waste time puzzling over this question.

V

Such monks always posed the most intriguing challenge. I loved to watch them squirm against my magnetism, fasting, even flagellating their backs with cords until the flesh was raw and bleeding, and then inevitably succumbing to my powers. I possessed them—sexually, emotionally, spiritually. But when I considered making them like me—for I had come to understand this possibility—I despised them too much to have them as companions. Still, I never grew tired of seeking a companion or torturing my prey, especially those who were particularly unworthy of me.

Once I'd observed Michael long enough to know that invariably he lifted weights on Monday, Wednesday, and Friday evenings, I started showing up in the workout room at the same times. At first, I only nodded to him and went about my workout (a joke, really, since to me the free weights might have been made of cork rather than steel). But one night, after a couple of the other monks had finished their workouts and left the room, I spoke.

"You know," I said, turning my head from the bench press after replacing the barbell on its rest. "You should not worry so much about Luke. You can't keep him from worldly dangers."

Without looking at me, Michael continued working the leg lift, his calves bulging into balls of olive flesh. Though the basement was cool, he wore only shorts and a tank top, soaked with perspiration. His dark, normally unkempt hair was tied back, accentuating his noble forehead, classic nose, and sturdy chin. He reminded me of the best of the Roman gladiators, one fiercely flaring his nostrils, searing his gaze into the eyes of his opponent, and yet alert to sudden moves.

"I know you want to protect him," I persisted.

"Why should you care what I think?" He glanced coldly at me, then returned his attention to exercise.

His spiritedness only aroused my admiration. I looked him

V

over as though he were a rare jeweled goblet, while he pretended to ignore my attention.

"None of us is above sin. True, good Brother?"

"None of us." He stopped, glaring at me. "I'm not pretending to be superior."

"Of course not."

"Some people are impressionable, that's all. They should be
left alone."

"I think you do consider yourself superior." I sat up on the
bench and faced him. "You're even above this kind of conversation, aren't you? I'll wager you've never had one quite like it
within the walls of this monastery."

"I can't say that I have." He resumed his lifts, straining to
speak as he raised the bar with his feet. "You don't care much for
our Rule, do you? Surely, your own community had a similar
one. How could you have made your peace with it?"

I laughed. "Now I see. You like me. You really do. Yes,
Michael, I am worldly. But it doesn't mean I belong to the world.
Oh, it sounds like a contradiction, I know. To crave things of the
flesh, but to be above them. But that's exactly my position. And
I relish it."

"You mock the spirit of monasticism. We're to live in the
world, but not be of it. That doesn't mean giving in to bodily
cravings, or believing we're above them." His emotion fueled an
acceleration in his lifts.

"I didn't say I was above the cravings. I'm above this world."

He stopped, his chest heaving from the workout, and
swiveled around on his bench to face me, his dark eyes intense.
"You believe that, don't you? You're not just trying to scandalize
me. But you're wrong, Brother Victor. You do belong to this
world. So much so that you frighten me."

"Frighten you?" I grinned. "I'm flattered."

Michael Schiefelbein

V

"Don't be. It says a lot more about me than you." Michael stood and grabbed a towel from a shelf above the weight bench and wiped his face and neck. "I have to shower before compline." He started toward the door.

I grabbed his wrist. "You're hard on yourself," I said. "But not by nature. That's why I like you." I smiled.

He studied me apprehensively and left the room.

That night, long after midnight, I crept down the dark dormitory corridor to his cell. The heavy door creaked on its hinges as I entered, but he did not stir in his bed. For several minutes I gazed at his form in a darkness that, in my gifted vision, borrowed the shades of dusk, not moonless night. He lay enshrouded in shadows, breathing with the regular rhythm of one whose conscience is clear. He lay on his side, his arm outside the wool blanket, his hair splashing the white sheets with black. Stooping and touching his shoulder, I entered the dream, which, though buried far beneath his consciousness, played as vividly before my eyes as my own memories.

"Come to me, Michael," I whispered, in spite of myself. "Don't fear the darkness. What kind of eternity awaits you in the light but one on bended knee? Would you fight your pride beyond the end of time?"

He moaned, opened his eyes and peered into mine, then slipped into a profound sleep.

III
Communications

Eleven

Rivulets of blood from the thorns stream down his ashen face. He shifts his weight to his feet in order to breathe and, when his strength fails him, hangs from his hands once again, the nails tearing his flesh. I remember taking those hands in mine one day on a fishing boat. Then they were browned by the sun, calloused from what I called his quaint profession as a builder.

"Victor," he says, his head rolling until his pained gaze falls on me, "God can forgive you." This is the way he always begins our conversations, no matter what scene of our lives together we are revisiting.

"God be damned! What kind of god lets them do this to you? He delights in your torture." I am standing beneath the

V

cross, alone, under a graphite sky, my cape whipped by the wind.

"No." He swallows and takes a breath, straining to support himself on his feet. "It's salvation. To give to the end. To give all, even your life."

"Why do you spew this rubbish at me, Joshu? You heard the rogue there next to you. Save yourself. Ask this god of yours for mercy, if that's what it takes. Don't pant and bleed here in front of me, with excrement running down your legs, telling me to ask for forgiveness from your god. Your god disgusts me. You disgust me."

"I…I love you, Victor."

"Yes, so you say. Every time we speak. Every time, damn you. And for the millionth time I answer, 'Come to me then.' I know you have a power. Not the power the mobs see, your flimsy healings and exorcisms. You know what I mean. The power derived from immortality. Power like mine. Why choose the world of light? What is its reward? Look what I have in the night. Eternity, mastery."

"Loneliness, longing."

"I satisfy my longings! Every one of them. And as for loneliness…company be damned when it takes the form of sniveling humans or a tyrant god who can't stand to share his power. But you, Joshu," I press my lips against his bloody feet and savor his taste, "you are different. We could spend eternity together in the night, having all we want."

Joshu gasps for breath and collects his strength to stand once again. "If you want me, you want the God of light. My God, my God." His eyes roll toward the threatening sky, ripped by lightning.

"No!" I scream. "Not again." I pound the cross with my fist. "Curse your god and live!"

"This is my body…body…body." The words reverberate through darkness now. The winds cease. I feel myself spinning. I open my eyes and once again find myself in the choir stall. The

Michael Schiefelbein

V

fool priest is consecrating the wafer. "This is my body, which will be given up for you," he says, with gravity. I want to storm to the altar and rip the host from his hands. I want to tear open his throat. But I restrain myself, forced to take part in the mockery until the host is in my mouth. Then I defile it by swallowing, letting it mix in my stomach with the blood of my victims, and vomiting it up before climbing into my coffin.

Twelve

My visions of Joshu were nothing new. They'd haunted me for 20 centuries. I hoped, though, as always upon moving into a new monastery, that they would cease. The crucifixion vision, especially, ripped at my heart. Although I had caused countless deaths, lapping up the blood that surfaced on taut flesh like vintage wine streaming from a cask, to see Joshu's death, Joshu's blood, was to relive my loss.

As much as I wished the visions would cease, I also feared this possibility. After all, the visions were all I had of Joshu. In them I felt that he was present, speaking, and not just a shadow created by my supernatural mind, felt that the risen Joshu communicated through this medium.

V

That there had to be such a medium at all exasperated me beyond endurance. It was like speaking through glass: The same cold matter that brought him near to me also, cruelly, formed an impenetrable barrier. The nearness to intimacy wrenched my heart.

The visions were induced by the chants and scents of Mass, and by feeding on the exceptionally rich blood of those who ate large quantities of meat—in the case of the mountain people, squirrel and porcupine and raccoon.

The visions also sometimes occurred while I studied volumes from my collection of ancient texts about Joshu: Some people called them the Apocrypha, but I knew from the lips of Joshu himself that much of the lore was true, tales about Joshu as a boy, breathing life into clay doves, striking down neighborhood bullies with a glance, healing wounded pets.

During our mountain hikes and sailing adventures Joshu would laugh over his youthful impetuosity. Not sure of what to make of his extraordinary powers at the time—whether he invented them or truly possessed them—but disinclined to reflect overly much, I would clap his naked back and say that he should use his powers. If he restrained his true nature, it would come out in one way or another.

Indeed, his power did come out, in the fire behind his words to temple officials, in his fury over injustices to toothless widows and snotty-nosed children. Compassion was his power, at the very core of his nature. This is what intrigued me about him: His compassion was not the result of pious submission to his god, but, in some inexplicable way, his very nature.

The visions also overcame me as I studied occult texts, which for many centuries were banned by the Church, though they could always be gotten from devious monks. Now such volumes were readily available in most monastic libraries. Mythology and satanism were now deemed legitimate fields of research by the

V

new, sophisticated, incorruptible brand of monk.

I can't say how the authors of these volumes learned of the world of darkness, whether they were inspired by court members like Tiresia, whether they themselves were vampires like me. But I was convinced of their accuracy. From them, I pieced together the components of my world, my history, my fate.

Certain fallen angels, followers of Lucifer, had escaped hell and fled to a kingdom near the moon where they thrived on their lust for power. A hierarchy was established, the angel Principia becoming queen, Copulus and Demitria her consorts, and the others her court.

These beings were driven to extend their kingdom beyond themselves to the mortal world, created in time. Principia, assuming the form of a buxom wench, charmed an Aryan chieftain. As he lay on her, sucking at her breast, he was transformed as I was transformed by Tiresia.

The chieftain lived, solitary and hungry for blood, as I lived, foraging by night among robust villagers for his food, creeping by day into a burial chamber.

All the while the court above watched him from their dark realm, waiting for him to pass his gifts to another and enter their ranks, only to have the new creature of darkness join them in his turn—if he so chose. For there was a choice.

I knew this not only because of Joshu's words to me, but from the ancient writers' stories about weak vampires who caved into the demands of the possessive god of light. They had their tempting visions too, it seemed, long before Joshu. Which agents of the world of light appeared to them, I ever sought to discover in the books, though so far unsuccessfully. But I had learned much of the dark realm and delighted in discovering even more.

One fact in particular came to dominate my thoughts over

V

the centuries. Bonds between members of the dark court were forged by mutual desire. When a vampire decided once and for all in favor of darkness, and created another soul of the night, he entered a world where he would no longer be alone. Long before I reached St. Thomas, I'd become determined to create my successor and move on to the dark realm, to be joined later, for eternity, by the vampire I'd created.

I had no delusions that Joshu could take that role. Once a spirit passed to the Kingdom of Light or the Kingdom of Darkness, the movement was final. So I lived for my communications with Joshu, as maddening as they were, until I could find one to replace him. Over the ages, as I toyed with pathetic young monks the way a cat cuffs and claws rodents, and as I defiled everything sacred with my lust and killings, I searched for a replica of Joshu—the one who obsessed me. Again and again my candidates disappointed me, as soon as they submitted to me. That ruined them, like a fissure ruins the blade of a sword.

Still, my obsession persisted.

Thirteen

One spring evening after compline, I willed young Luke to my cell. His blond shaggy locks had tumbled endearingly over his brow as he'd chanted the psalm. His pale face and hands had seemed almost translucent under the lights. The effort it took to summon him was nothing, barely the amount of concentration required for lacing a shoe. Fifteen minutes after the Grand Silence began, he tapped on my door.

"Enter." Having pulled off my robe, I lay stretched out on the bed.

The lamplight threw his lean shadow on the wall as he closed the door behind him. With an impatient wave I bid him come to me. He timidly approached the bed.

V

"What took you so long, boy?"

"I came as fast as I could, Victor. Brother Matthew was walking up and down the dormitory hallway. I had to wait."

"Why are you lying?" I pulled him to the bed by his cowl and brought his face inches from mine.

"I'm not."

"Get out." I released his robe.

"No, please, Victor." He touched my cheek. "Don't make me go again. We ain't done nothing for weeks."

"Why is that, Luke?" I eyed the cowering boy with disgust. "Well?"

"My confession," he admitted. He lowered his eyes and then turned them imploringly on me. "But I told you, it's the guilt. When you sin against celibacy, it's like you're unfaithful to the Lord. I can't help confessing. The guilt just eats away at me. Old Brother Joseph ain't gonna tell anyone anyway. He'd never break the confessional seal. Besides, he's heard it all before."

"From your friends Peter and Gerard, no doubt." I'd written off the effete pair of monks as not worth raping the moment I set eyes on them.

"It's just common here, that's all."

"You've whored ever since you set foot in this place, haven't you, boy?"

"It was different. It was never like this."

"Like what?"

Luke's eyes gleamed and he smiled like a child dying to share a secret. He sat on the edge of the bed. I leaned back, my hands behind my head.

"I always knew I was different, Victor. When I was little, there was this farmhand of ours. He'd work in the field and come back all sweaty. He'd take his shirt off and wash himself down at the pump outside. I'd stand inside the screen door and

V

look at him, my heart pumping away like an engine. I didn't know anything about what I was feeling except it was good. He'd bring me a stick of gum or some licorice. Sometimes he'd skip rocks with me across the creek on our place. My grandaddy was too old to do much with me and all my brothers was raised and married." Luke lifted my legs and, scooting back against the wall, laid them in his lap.

"So anyway. I took a shining to Bud—that was his name. Used to dream he was holding me in his big ol' hairy arms, kissing me. I knew that wasn't right. But I woke up feeling good all the same. Then he got work down at Chattanooga. Left us after harvest.

"I tell you, Victor, I liked to have died. Was sick to my stomach. Couldn't eat. My grandaddy sent me into town to see the doctor. He said there wasn't nothing wrong with me. Granddaddy about beat me senseless for pretending. Course I couldn't say nothing to nobody.

"I got over Bud in time, but the whole thing started me seeing things different. Here I was, 14 years old and never had no interest in girls. I noticed how good the other field hands started looking. Played around with one in the barn. Knew it couldn't be right so I went to confession."

"Your first mistake." The story was starting to bore me, but since he was working up to his paean to me, I humored him.

Luke sighed and shook his head. He rested it against the wall and stared at the ceiling. "Man, that priest gave it to me bad. Told me sleepin' with another man was worse than murder. Said if you died with that on your soul, you'd go to the deepest part of hell. Gave me a penance that would have worn out a saint."

"And you took it to heart, of course."

"Yes, sir, I took it to heart. Started praying that I'd shake off these feelings for men. Started going to morning Mass in town—had to walk two miles to get there, sometimes in snow

Michael Schiefelbein

V

and ice. Started talking to the priest about living a holy life. Before you knew it, I was in the novitiate here at St. Thomas—right out of high school. Then..." He hesitated and lowered his eyes as though saddened by what came next.

"Then you saw that the feelings got even stronger here. You were surrounded by beautiful men and thought you were in heaven." I had heard this confession many times.

"I got desperate. I ended up going to bed with a couple monks. But I fasted, prayed. Mike helped me."

"Brother Michael?" The boy had my attention now.

Luke nodded his head. "When I told him about the temptations, he said he had 'em too. Said we could help each other out."

"Yes, I'll bet."

"No, Victor. It wasn't like that. I thought he was good-looking, but we never fooled around. He was too strong. We'd pray together. We'd talk while we worked on the grounds and in the greenhouse. I dunno, it was like I could keep the feelings down then. Like they were channeled into a new path."

"Touching," I said.

"It was all going OK until you showed up. I wanted you bad. You was so confident and good-looking. You didn't seem to give a damn about rules. I never thought of things the way you did. Questioning, I mean. I never rebelled against the Church. It's like, when I'm with you, it don't seem like my feelings are bad. It's like God sent you for me."

I chuckled at this. "So that's why you run off to confession regularly."

Luke's face grew serious. "I ain't saying I've got it all under control. I ain't completely changed. It's mostly when we're apart, afterwards. Then I start worrying that maybe I have sinned."

"Maybe you have."

"What do you mean?"

V

I smiled at the panic in Luke's voice. "Maybe it is a sin. Maybe you'll wind up in hell."

"You don't really believe that, Victor. I know you don't."

"Think what you like. It's getting late. You better go." I wanted to feed and it was nearly midnight.

"Not yet." Luke grinned, got up on his hands and knees and buried his face in my crotch.

My cock hardened. Although I stopped ejaculating after my night existence began, sex gave me great pleasure, mostly the pleasure of having power over the human kneeling to lick my balls or take me in his ass. My whole body still shuddered with orgasms, but now it was my mind that exploded—in a dizzying euphoria of colors and sounds.

I stripped Luke of his clothes. I inspected his slight body, hairless and soft, his long slender cock protruding from a mass of blond fur. Throwing him face down on the rug, I mounted him. But I had barely entered him when I suddenly lost interest in the white body splayed before me. It was too easy. He wanted me too much. I felt no resistance in his will.

"Go to bed," I said, getting up and throwing on my robe.

"What's the matter, Victor?" He rolled over, still erect and badly wanting me.

"Another time, not tonight."

"Did I say something wrong? Do you want something else?" He clutched my arm like a beggar.

"Leave me."

Crestfallen, he dressed. I let him kiss my lips before he left the cell.

By now I was weak with hunger. In the heavy rain, I squished through the muddy grounds of the monastery toward the trees, invisible in the darkness to mortals, but to me a line of grayish branches, still leafless. Just inside the woods, I froze in

V

place. I sensed a human within a stone's throw from me. My fangs instantly grew. My breathing became as excited and loud as that of a bull ready to charge. Someone lurked among the trees. I could stalk him, but as famished as I was it could only be to feed, and if the spy was a monk, I would endanger my position at St. Thomas. While I still had some power of discernment, I sped through the forest, as fast as my thoughts could carry me. My legs moved not at all now, but with the velocity of a jet I was carried bodily through the woods, my body dodging trees and brambles as though it carried its own radar system.

My senses guided me to a shack, like those of all my other victims in the mountains. The windows were dark, but the chimney smoked. The rotting door gave with a slight tug. Inside, the uneven floor moaned beneath my weight. The light from the fire painted the sticks of furniture orange. The room smelled of cat urine and damp upholstery.

"Who's out there?" an old woman demanded from the bedroom. "I got a gun in here, and I ain't afraid to use it."

Her delicious scent overwhelmed me. My nostrils dilated to catch her flavor. When I entered her door, she was standing near the bed, aiming a shotgun at me.

"Hello, Granny." I advanced, and she started trembling.

"Get out of my house else I'll blow you out."

"Now, that wouldn't do."

Before I could take another step, she fired. The bullet passed through my stomach and out my back, stunning me only momentarily. In an instant the pain dissipated, the wound closing as though my flesh were liquid and the projectile had only briefly parted the waters.

"Please!" She dropped the gun and sank to her knees. "Oh, please leave me be."

I approached her, lifting her chin to look into her rheumy

V

eyes. "Good night, Granny." With a quick twist, I snapped her neck, a merciful gesture as I saw it, and picked her up to sink my fangs into her throat. It is only a myth that vampires cannot drink from corpses; they can, as long as the blood stays warm. Her loose skin tore easily and I fed on her rich old blood for nearly a quarter of an hour, I was so hungry.

After disposing of her body beneath a pair of fallen trees, I trekked up the mountainside to a clearing for a view of the valley. Below, the monastery rested in darkness, except for a few faint lights. Who was up at this time of night? Who had been watching me in the woods? Perhaps only Luke, who couldn't bear to leave me. But the presence I felt there was a stronger one than his, one I did not sense again as I crossed the monastery grounds but one I would attune myself to in the future.

Fourteen

The balmy nights of May brought with them a keen loneliness, for during the whole month I was bereft of contact with Joshu. Luke, who had amused me for a while, now satisfied me less and less. Still, he proved useful for learning more about the monk who did intrigue me.

One night when I did not find Michael in the weight room I wandered to the greenhouse. The lights there annoyed me, but I shaded my eyes and strolled quietly toward voices that rose above the rows of plants grown to raise money for the monastery. (The plants were transported to a market in Knoxville.) Concealed behind a wall of tall ficus, I listened to the conversation between Michael and Luke.

V

"It is different, Mike. God, I can't explain it. It's not like the other times. Why don't you just lay off!"

"What are we about here, Luke? You can argue for that kind of love all you want. For the sake of argument, let's say you're right. Homosexual love is legitimate. Even so, you're a monk. You took a vow of celibacy."

"That's when I thought I'd go straight to hell if I didn't kill the urges. Hell, Mike, I don't wanna kill 'em when I'm with him. It's like it's a sign from God or something."

One of the two took a few steps, and I drew back behind the foliage.

"You want to know what a sign from God is?" Michael sounded impatient. "Good fruit. Remember when Jesus says you'll know them by their fruit?"

"Hell, yes. And that's exactly right. God is love, right? That's what we have, Victor and me. Where two or three are gathered and all that, you know. I understand it now."

"Attractions are deceptive, Luke. Attractions don't mean love. Why do you think you still feel guilty? You think if this little affair were such a good thing, you'd be heading to confession all the time?"

"You're pissing me off."

"I'm telling you the truth."

"It's just the old shit." Luke nearly shouted, but he seemed to collect himself, lowering his voice. "God don't send guilt trips. Brother Matthew said so himself. Lotsa times, they're from the devil. He gets a person all tied up in knots to do his dirty work."

"If he were good," Michael implored, "if he were good and if the love were pure…Luke, don't you see this is exactly how Satan works, not through what seems grotesque and repulsive, but through what seduces us. That's what I'm trying to tell you: The man has seduced you. He has no love to give you."

Michael Schiefelbein

V

"You'd take away the only joy I ever had, wouldn't you?" Luke sounded choked-up now. "Here I thought you was my friend."

"He doesn't give a damn about you. Open your eyes." Michael's voice quivered, perhaps as he shook Luke by the shoulders—the plants blocked my view.

"He wants me. Don't look at me like that, damn you. I ain't crazy. Don't you think I know when someone wants me?"

"For what, Luke? For what? It's some power game he's playing. He likes to have people under his thumb."

"You know what I think? I think you're as jealous as all get out. Someone else takes a shine to me, and you go bananas. That's what it is. You like to play like some high and mighty judge. But you're in the game too."

A definite hit on the part of young Luke, I thought. I waited for Michael to go on the defensive. His response was a pleasant surprise.

"Maybe I am jealous." He spoke softly, seriously. "Maybe I envy this intimacy you feel, the physical affection. Maybe I feel Victor's power myself. But that only confirms what I'm saying to you. You don't seduce someone you love. This is his mode of operating."

"So that makes him Satan? Maybe it's the only way he knows." Michael sighed, defeated. "Maybe it is."

That night after compline, Michael remained kneeling in the dark. I remained, too. A cross-breeze from the opened windows carried in sweet smells of lilacs and irises blooming in the courtyard.

I willed him to cross the chapel to me, but he resisted. His own will pressed upon my chest like hands keeping me at bay. But his bowed head, his kneeling form betrayed no hint of struggle, he was so composed. Suddenly he looked up, recognized me in the shadows, and spoke.

"Where are you from?"

"Many places. England was the last place. Brother Matthew

V

told the community all about me, didn't he?"

"Why did you become a monk?"

I smiled. "If it's a heart-to-heart you want, Michael, perhaps we should adjourn to my cell, if you don't mind violating the Grand Silence."

"Did you listen to the reading tonight? 'The Lord has given an opportunity of repentance to all who would return to him.'"

"Yes, Clement of Rome waxes on, doesn't he?"

"The words didn't faze you."

I crossed the aisle and stood before him where he knelt. "You're not a prig, Michael. And you're not as self-righteous as you sound. So why are you preaching to me? What is it that possesses you? Surely it's more than the love for your friend." I touched his hand. He pulled it away and stood. We were so close I could smell the wine from dinner on his breath.

"I have a responsibility to Luke. If he won't listen to reason, I'll have to go to the abbot. It's my duty. I'm telling you so you'll back off."

"He's like a brother to you, eh?"

"He is my brother. So are you."

"Funny, I don't feel like your brother."

He started to turn away, but I grabbed his firm arm. "You're intelligent, Michael. Surely you don't take all this too seriously." I waved toward the chapel, as though it were a world rather than a room. "Dogmatism, I mean. Human rules, penances, busy rituals. Surely for you spirituality is something more…how should I put it…elastic, expansive, spontaneous. God speaks to each soul in a different way, don't you think?"

"Yes, he does. And I know his voice when I hear it." He jerked his arm away.

"Ah. One of the fortunate ones. The chosen few. You can discern good from evil, like hot and cold. No warm for you. Perhaps

V

my first assessment of you was wrong after all. Perhaps you are self-righteous." As he walked away from me, I called after him, "If you run into Luke, tell him I'll be waiting for him in my cell."

Fifteen

My father was a true paterfamilias. As a Roman patriarch, he ruled his sons and his sons' families by the laws of practicality, reserving sentiment for private moments with my mother. Embedded in my memory is the sight of my youngest brother, Justin, sick with fever after serving in a provincial regiment. Moaning in pain, he lay naked on his cot, his youthful body still firm and muscular but writhing now, his eyes glazed, his face pallid as the linens. My father, a senator, was involved at the time with some important state matters that required careful attention. My mother, exhausted from attending Justin, was in danger of nervous collapse. I was home on leave from Palestine, but family business occupied my time. My other brothers, both

V

officers, were stationed abroad.

"What are his chances?" My father had taken the physician and me outside my brother's room, away from my mother. Still fit and straight of carriage at the age of 60, my father was a fierce-looking man. His cold blue eyes, focused on the physician, gazed intensely from beneath a wide brow.

The old physician, a bald curmudgeon with a great beak of a nose and thin lips, scratched his chin. "I have seen this fever before in those returning from the provinces in the far south. If he survives it, his mind will be touched. If not, he will die within the week."

My father hesitated not one second. "In that case, it must end. Today, no later. Take care of the matter in haste. Let my wife learn nothing of it."

The physician bowed and disappeared. Immediately my mother, who'd been eavesdropping, rushed to the corridor and fell in hysterics at my father's feet, a bundle of white robes.

"No, Lucretius, I beg of you. Let him live. Do not take him from me." Justin, who had her fine features and high cheekbones, was her favorite son.

"What would you have, woman?" My father's face remained immobile. "Unbearable pain for him, madness if he's unlucky enough to live?"

"I will tend to him myself," she said, grabbing his legs, her reddened eyes turned up to him. "You needn't waste one moment here."

"You have duties, Lydia." Her emotion only made my father speak more sternly. "Now release me."

Mother collapsed into a heap, sobbing violently.

Following my father's lead, I ignored her and accompanied him to his rooms to discuss business matters needing urgent attention.

"She will recover," he said as we crossed the courtyard,

V

which was gleaming in the midday sun. "And so shall we."

Recover he might, but for three days and three nights after my brother's funeral rites he locked himself in his rooms. As for myself, though I shed not a single tear in public, though I reprimanded my mother for her tears, I knew for the first time the emptiness that a final death, a mortal's death, brings. Especially when it is your own flesh and blood whom Charon ferries across the river Styx to the Underworld—a boy you taught to ride, to handle a sword, to swear admirably.

For some reason, after my chapel interview with Michael, my mind returned to the scene of my brother's fever and my father's pragmatic decision. Cold blood guaranteed survival, not only of an individual, but of a people. Certainly a vampire needed it.

I was not given to brooding, but in certain periods the isolation that was the fruit of such coldness, the isolation of centuries, came over me like a blanket of darkness that even my sight could not pierce. In moments like these, I rallied my spirit by dreaming of the time when, after entering the realm of night, I would be joined by whomever I had chosen on earth, a beloved who would wipe away all thoughts of Joshu.

In the meantime, I took comfort where I could. That night I willed Luke to my cell. With a flashlight to guide us—for Luke's sake—we hiked out to the woods, to a spot cleared by mountain dwellers, and rested against a stump overgrown with vines. Along the way he asked me questions about the Church with an interest, an ebullience, of one who never previously conceived of the possibility of questioning.

"What do you mean the Church's power is arbitrary?" he asked, cradling my head in his lap. Around us a warm breeze rustled the branches and cicadas whirred.

"I mean the Pope's a foolish old man who invents laws."

"But he's the Vicar of Christ."

V

"He's nothing. He knows nothing of Christ but the wives' tales passed on about him by ignorant fishermen and tent-makers."

"But didn't Christ call Peter to feed his sheep?"

"Your Christ, the Church's Christ, is a god made in the image of effete men who've never had a good fuck in their lives, or if they have, who've thrashed themselves with whips to relieve their guilt. They hate their own cocks so much they'd light votive candles to make them fall off, if it would do the trick. Good old Origen, revered Church Father that he was, castrated himself. Did you know that?"

"Shit!" Luke winced.

"Virgins. Celibates. What kind of god makes bodies and forbids you to use them? And makes you feel holy and superior when you do manage to turn into gutless, passionless stone?"

"But Jesus didn't—"

"He worshiped a demented god. He was deluded." I stood. "Let's get off this subject. Before I tear off someone's head."

"If you feel this way, Victor," Luke timidly pursued, "how come you ended up in a monastery?"

I picked up a fallen branch and cracked it against the stump with such force that the sound reported like shotgun fire. "It is my mission, damn you! We hear the gospel every day. Well, I have my own gospel, the true gospel. Not the one that serves a possessive, tyrannical god, but one that frees us from submission to him. I live it. Daily. Why grovel at his feet for eternity? Do you want an eternity on your goddamned knees?"

"Jesus said God is our father." The boy was frightened by my outburst. For all his delight in unorthodox talk, I had gone too far.

"I am your father." I fell on the boy, worked up his habit, and with only the dew for lubrication, forced myself into him. He groaned in pain at first, then in pleasure as I rode him.

In that moment I wanted his blood more than ever.

V

Nuzzling my face against his throat, I heard the blood pumping through his jugular as loud as a bass drum. My fangs descended. I bared them. They grazed his soft skin, barely scratching its surface, before I jerked my head away, just as my thrusting body brought him to his climax.

"God, I love you, Victor." He panted the words.

"Go back. I need to walk. Alone." I got up and disappeared into the woods before he had time to protest. My urge for food had suddenly driven me to near-insanity. Spotting a raccoon nosing the carcass of an animal, I rushed to it, grasped its furry throat, and sank my fangs into its tough hide. I sucked every drop of gamy blood from its veins and hurled the hairy mass against a tree.

Just before dawn, tired from aimless tramping about the woods, I crawled into the mausoleum and settled into my pine bed. Exhausted, I drifted toward a welcome sleep, when my eyes snapped open. Someone lurked outside the tomb, someone strong and unafraid—I felt such a presence within my bowels. Then I smiled and closed my eyes.

Michael Schiefelbein

IV
Clearing the Path

Sixteen

Brother Matthew stood before the communion rail, the saints in all their glory inspecting the crown of his balding head from their niches in the high altar. He removed his wire-frame spectacles and rubbed his close-set eyes. "This isn't the best time of day for serious news," he said, "but it is one of the few times we're all gathered together."

All 23 monks had remained in their stalls after compline, which had been moved to 10 o'clock to accommodate me during the summer months when the shadows of dusk didn't collect until after 9. A couple of the older bastards regularly nodded off before the final blessing, and they had to be nudged now.

"It looks like there've been some break-ins up in the hills.

V

The police aren't sure what the motive is. As you know, the folks up there have no valuables to speak of. They're also as isolated as can be, so we're not even sure why anyone would wander around up there." Matthew replaced his glasses, clasped his hands, and rocked nervously back and forth. "It seems some people have abandoned their houses. Brother George and Brother Michael first noticed that several months ago."

I glanced across the aisle at Michael, whose dark hair, pulled back into a ponytail, gleamed after his post-workout shower. He was all intensity, scratching his new goatee, studying the abbot as though he were pondering metaphysics rather than the disappearance of hillbillies.

"As you know, it's nothing new for people to move down to the city's shelters during the winter months to get out of the cold, so at first no one was alarmed. Then relatives put in missing person reports. And the disappearances continued when the weather warmed up. The county police started to investigate. Of course you can imagine how seriously they pursued trudging through mountain thickets to investigate the cases of missing indigent people."

Several of the monks shook their heads or mumbled something about the shame of it.

"However," Brother Matthew continued, "earlier this week they found a body."

A rumble of voices echoed through the chapel.

"Brother George, perhaps you would like to take it from here." The abbot turned to Brother George, a short, middle-aged man who managed the community's finances and was second in command after Matthew. His silver hair, clipped close to his skull, fuzzed the outline of his squarish head. He stood to address the group, and the abbot rested against the communion rail.

"You all know that the monastery regularly sends food to

some of the mountain folks." His voice was a deep, gravelly smoker's voice. "Well, Michael and I got worried when one of our regulars disappeared without a trace—an older woman with no family, practically lame in one foot and with no transportation. We searched the woods ourselves, thinking maybe she fell and hurt herself. At first we didn't see any sign of her. Then we noticed a trail of something—it could have been blood—leading up to a fallen tree, a big oak about five feet around. It was strange since how could she have gotten under it? But we got the police out here a couple days ago. They sent for a crew of workers with a crane. They found her body under it. Molly Spaker was her name. Nice old woman. Husband died last year. He was a miner from up in Kentucky."

"How did she get under the tree?" Brother Alfred asked the question, a swarthy man at St. Thomas to complete a book on some drivel in Aquinas's *Summa Theologiae*.

"They don't have a clue," George answered. "But evidently her neck was broken. And, well, I might as well say it—her blood was drained."

The chapel buzzed with murmurs.

The abbot stood, looking grave. "The concern here is that some psychopath is on the loose in the woods. The police are continuing their search for the missing folks, with the help of our information about them. And they're hunting for the killer of Mrs. Spaker. In the meantime, we've got to tighten our own security measures since we're obviously sitting ducks for a killer at large."

"That means all outside doors stay locked," Brother George threw in. "Please use your keys. And keep windows facing the exterior of the monastery shut. If you open your transoms, the interior courtyard windows should keep your rooms cool."

"We probably have nothing to worry about," the abbot continued. "If someone had wanted one of us, they could have had

V

him by now. Probably, we're talking about someone smart enough to pick victims who wouldn't be missed."

The monks for the most part were not gossips—scholars rarely are, content to keep the world at bay while they bury themselves in their studies—but several of the monks did whisper together in the foyer after we had prayed for the deceased and for the apprehension of the murderer, apparently feeling the Grand Silence warranted violation under the circumstances. The shadows of the robed men rose like spirits on the walls.

I retraced my steps through the chapel to get to the library, where I could bury myself in books and stew over the matters at hand. The antechamber to the stacks was a large room whose beamed ceiling rose to a height of 40 feet, the vast space corresponding to five levels of stacks on the other side of one wall. Against tall wainscoting, study desks of darkened oak were arranged around a block of reference shelves in the center of the room.

I took a seat at one of the desks against an external wall where two arched windows framed the woods and distant mountaintops in the daylight, but in the darkness formed two blank eyes. Yellow lamplight fell upon the volume I'd left on the desk, a study of the historical Jesus, the result of some ambitious theology professor's drive for tenure, and for me, the opportunity to dream of Joshu.

The words blurred as I read, the page becoming like a theater curtain of transparent gauze that melts away when the lights behind it reveal a set and movement on the stage. I saw the mangled old woman crumpled on the linoleum. *Nothing can be linked to me,* I said to myself. *The woman's body, the blood, the superhuman effort to move the tree—none of these points a finger to me. But I must find new grounds for feedings. Down in the city perhaps, among Knoxville's poor neighborhoods, in the prison out-*

Michael Schiefelbein

V

side the town's limits. Less convenient of course, especially now when my lust for the blood of young Luke makes it hard to resist sinking my fangs into his throat. But necessary all the same.

"Good evening, Brother Victor." The voice of the abbot broke through my thoughts. He looked a bit uncomfortable. "I hate to break the Grand Silence, but I do have something important to discuss with you, something I've been putting off, and with all this horrible stuff going on—well, there's not much silence right now anyway. May I?" He nodded to a chair near the desk.

"Please."

"What is it you're reading?"

"Nothing of interest. What's on your mind?"

He shifted and removed his glasses, studying them as he spoke. "Something's been brought to my attention, regarding you and Brother Luke."

"What's that?"

"At the risk of taking our friend Thomas à Kempis too seriously"—he looked up now as though to say I ought not take him too seriously either—"it's about particular friendship."

"Becoming too close to one person in the community."

"Yes. It's an old-fashioned idea of course. But there's something to be said for it." Perhaps detecting the disdain in my voice, he became emboldened enough to look me in the eye.

"I'm all for old-fashioned ideas, Brother Matthew."

"That's good, because I do believe this is a serious matter. Luke is...what can I say. He's naïve in the extreme. He's not bright either—very impressionable. You, well, I take it you've seen some of the world."

"What makes you think so?"

"Oh, I'm not sure. The way you carry yourself. The way you speak. I guess it's just an impression."

"I see."

V

"But at any rate, you're older. He's hardly out of his teens. Luke needs to be handled delicately."

"Protected, you mean? From more experienced people?"

Frustrated, the abbot rubbed his cheek. "Of course experienced people have a lot to teach a boy like Luke. That wisdom, the right way to handle feelings, etcetera, that's something he should learn about."

"The boy's infatuated, Brother. He's young. It happens. I'll take care of it."

"Very good." He stood to go, but turned back to me as though a bit dissatisfied with the turn our conversation had taken. "I hope you'll take my advice in the right spirit. I don't want to seem inhospitable to a brother who's been through a tragedy. I can see why you would reach out for a friend."

"You're kind, Brother. Good night." I turned my attention to my book. He hesitated a second, then left the room.

So Michael had carried out his threat. Of course, since our talk in the chapel, I had continued summoning Luke to my cell and we'd gone on with our nocturnal romps through the woods. For the most part young Luke's company amused me, took the edge off the solitude of the night. Granted, he offered me no challenge and never had. But before it got tedious, his kind of wide-eyed fawning entertained me for an hour or so. Besides, our liaison won me Michael's attention. Perhaps now, however, my strategy should change.

Later that week I made my move, after sucking on his tender cock in the woods—so excited by its engorgement that I would have pierced the nearly transparent membrane keeping me from the blood if I'd possessed an ounce less restraint. The full moon had already reached a western point in its arc back to the earth. Patches of its faint light lay on the rocks, vines, and bare earth the color of coffee grounds. Luke and I had thrown

Michael Schiefelbein

V

off our habits and, guided by a flashlight, treaded naked to the familiar clearing where we conducted our rendezvous. In the hollow of a tree he'd stashed a bottle of wine he'd filched from the dusty collection in the cellar—the daring boy he'd now become. He'd chugged a good amount of it before our playing began. Now his face was the shade of the wine, but instead of breaking his energy the drink pumped it through him. His slim, naked form paced restlessly as he rambled on and on about the stalker roaming the mountainside.

"You think he escaped from a loony bin? I believe there's one in Knoxville, or maybe it's Nashville. Wherever the hell. You know, it's a damn scary thing. Someone sucking out blood like that. That's what the coroner guy said, ain't it?"

I shrugged, bored with the topic, and lay my head back against the stump. I imagined the dim moon, bright to my sight, was the sun and that once again I was basking in its heat.

"That ol' gal musta died from shock before he even started sucking. You think? Tell you what, I wouldn't want to be the detective that's gotta go poking around for the rest of the bodies."

"Maybe there are no other bodies."

"Hell, where there's one, I'll lay odds there's a dozen. Like rats in a barn. Yessir, betcha anything some crazy man read too many vampire stories. Got hisself some spikey teeth and ripped into her." He finally stopped pacing, peering through the trees as though on the watch for the killer, and sprawled out next to me after he tossed the drained bottle into the thicket.

"You've got a morbid imagination tonight."

"I expect so." He had calmed himself now and laid his head on my shoulder, his blonde locks soft against my cheek. "Anyway, with you here, I feel pretty damn safe."

"The abbot spoke to me the other night, Luke. About us."

"What about us?" He spoke drowsily now.

V

"He said our liaison had to end. The man could make trouble, weakling that he is."

It took a moment before Luke could register the news. Then he lifted his head, his spirit rallied by the threat. "To hell with him. To hell with St. Thomas. It's time for us to get out of this place, Victor. We could get out of this hick state and head to a big city. San Francisco maybe. Hell, half the city's gay, according to a magazine I read. We could get us a house. You might could teach. I could tend to lawns and such." The pupils of his blue eyes dilated with his excitement.

"Like a dream come true, eh?"

"Yessir. Exactly."

"I'm afraid you'll have to live your dream with someone else."

"What? What do you mean?" His forehead wrinkled as though he were trying to discern whether I was joking or not.

"This is the end, that's all. You'll get over me." I got up and put on my robe. As I started to walk away, Luke sprang up and grabbed my arm.

"Damn, Victor, you're serious, ain't you? Why? What use have you got for this place? You hate the fucking Church. Jesus, Victor, you can't just pitch me like garbage. I love you."

I stared coldly into his panic-stricken eyes, jerked my arm free, and resumed walking.

"Don't you love me, Victor?" He called after me. "Don't you love me?" His voice broke into a sob. "You bastard! Goddamn you. You hear me? Goddamn you!"

As usual, my appetite for blood overpowered me after coming so close to Luke's veins—one reason for my abruptness, which was perhaps more severe than usual. But I couldn't hunt in the mountains, not now with county police scouting the area, so I headed west toward the city. Attuned to the scent of blood, my body lifted and soared through the humid June night to a farm-

V

house several miles down the road, still far outside the city. The two-story abode rose on a hill, above fields of tobacco, a weatherbeaten but sturdy structure. Inside a screened porch, I found the back door unlocked. A large calico cat, lounging on a dresser stripped of its drawers, watched me with curiosity as I entered.

The back door opened into a kitchen, where pots and pans lay piled on a drainboard and a table covered with a checkered cloth held a bowl of plastic fruit. Through a dining room, and a living room where a grandfather clock's pendulum ticked noisily, I followed the scent of blood. It became especially strong in the entrance hall. I mounted a staircase there, pausing at the top before a partially open door where I inhaled the rich odor of what I needed. But I advanced toward a second door where the smell was even stronger, more concentrated.

Bunk beds and another bed held three boys. The youngest, in the bottom bunk, couldn't have been more than three. The boy in the top bunk, his long lashes curling up against his cheeks, was probably 5 or 6. An older boy lay in the large bed, his sheet crumpled up at the foot, his tanned arms and legs dark against the linens. Through the open window, cicadas buzzed, but no breeze stirred the heavy summer air.

My chest was heaving now I needed blood so badly. My fangs were ready to tear flesh. But which child should I take? The youngest and most tender? The oldest and biggest portion? A pity it would have been to have two brothers awaken in the morning to find the third drained of life. I could take all three; they were small enough. But the parents in the next room would be left with nothing. I cursed the speck of human softness surfacing now. "Worry be damned," I muttered, clapping my hand over the oldest boy's mouth. His eyes flashed open. He tried to scream, and flapped against the mattress like a fish in the bottom of a boat. Within seconds I had pierced his throat and, draining most of his

V

blood, I quickly twisted his neck to end any lingering misery.

The youngest boy stirred, and for several seconds I remained frozen, inhaling the sweaty odor of my victim, the wet-dog scent that children get when they play outdoors. The child in the bottom bunk suddenly started to cry. I rushed to him and snapped his neck. With no time to drink in case the parents had stirred, and with my thirst already slaked, I bolted out the window and rode the thick, warm air back to the monastery.

Seventeen

Restless and sullen, and now lonelier than ever, I cursed Joshu again and again during the next month when he continued to not appear in a vision. I was sick of the inescapable fate of my feedings, sick of preying on drug addicts and prostitutes, people living on the streets in Knoxville. I resented being deprived of Luke, even though a better trophy required this sacrifice. I hadn't the patience for calculating ingenious ways to win Michael, and since he had kept a distance from me, I feared that my desire for an equal would go forever unmet.

Over the weeks Luke's reactions to my dismissal of him fluctuated as much as the whims of a Roman aristocrat's spoiled child. Initially, he slumped at the long dining room table with

V

lowered eyes, mechanically moving his spoon but eating little. In the chapel he held his breviary in front of his face so no one could see that his lips weren't moving to the psalms. When we filed into the corridor after compline, he dragged his feet despondently.

Then several times he rallied himself to plead his case. The first time I was lying on my cot, turning the brittle pages of an ancient tome on the Dark Kingdom—a book I'd discovered half a millennium before. Some ambitious vampire had written the Latin text, I was sure of that. I'd lit a few candles to rest my eyes from what for me was the painful light of the chapel. Before Luke could knock, I felt his weak presence outside the door.

"Come in, Luke," I called. I was lying on my side, my elbow against the bed, my head propped on my hand.

The door opened. His eyes were red. He wore his habit, but his feet were in slippers.

"Well, don't stand there. Come in and shut the door."

He followed my orders but continued to hover sheepishly near the door. "I couldn't sleep."

"How unfortunate." I turned the page to a drawing of a voluptuous woman swathed in an ermine mantle, high priestess of the Dark Kingdom.

"Victor, if you're tired of me, I could try some new things. To make you feel really good. I know I ain't that experienced. But hell, I'd be willing to take a shot at anything. You're a temperamental type. Just like a horse I had once. Wouldn't let you near him for days and then would eat out of your hand like a puppy." He forced a smile. "I know that's all there is to it. The abbot...hell, you have him under your thumb. He ain't gonna do nothing if you wanna stick around here. Maybe sometime, though, you'll wanna go. We could go anywhere, right? Sky's the limit."

"Come here, Luke." I patted the mattress.

He eagerly obeyed, sitting down on the bed. His body left

V

my book in shadow. I could smell tobacco on his habit. He'd started smoking, apparently to ease his misery.

"You're right. I am temperamental. I am weary of you. It can't be helped. There's nothing you can do. The best thing for you is to stop dreaming. Open your eyes. You're young. If you want to find love, get out of this perverse monastery and get yourself a lover. But don't expect anything from me. Now go to bed."

He started to tremble. His eyes welled and the tears tumbled down his face. "Damn, Victor. I can't put you out of my mind like you was some impure thought." He sobbed and then took a deep breath to collect himself. "I ain't never loved someone. I'd rather die than be without you." He grabbed my wrist.

"Then you'd better die, Luke. I'm telling you once and for all, you're a fool to hope."

He nodded his head dejectedly, rose, and slowly walked to the door.

"It's the best thing," I called after him.

There were a few more scenes like this one, then long letters blotched with tear stains, then angry outbursts during evening recreation, when in my boredom I would gravitate toward the common room. During one of those times he deliberately spilled his drink on me as I sat on the sofa, joking with one of the younger, better-looking brothers.

"Oh, I'm sorry, Brother," he said, with exaggerated remorse. "Hell, I'm clumsier than a blind old cat." He mopped my habit with his handkerchief.

"Never mind, Luke." I grabbed the handkerchief from him.

"Never mind? Hell no. I'm a damned good brother. I'm here to serve."

Two brothers seated near the piano interrupted their conversation at Luke's loud declaration, made, as best I could tell, with the help of a few glasses of wine. Michael, playing a board

V

game with Brother George, the administrator, also glanced up and comprehended the situation at once. When Luke tried to tug the handkerchief away from me, his eyes filling with angry tears, Michael came over and reasoned with him.

"Luke, why don't you come help me a minute in the greenhouse."

"To hell with the greenhouse." Luke's blue eyes stood out against his flushed cheeks. "To hell with you." He turned, stumbling against a chair, and charged out of the room.

"Maybe you should go help him," I said to Michael.

His dark eyes peered at me with uncertainty and reserve, but also with something more. "No, he's best left alone for now."

After another similar scene, and after the abbot counseled Luke that the end of our intimacy was for his good, Luke rebelled again, calling me a cocksucker in chapel. When he ventured to my cell later that night, drunkenly remorseful and eager to plead for my affection, I clutched him by his slender throat. His eyes widened in horror. The acne on his cheeks stood out like blue match heads against his white face.

"Listen to me, damn you. I'll kill you if you don't shut your mouth and stay out of my way." I flung him to the floor.

"Kill me then!" he sobbed, rubbing his neck.

When I lifted my foot to kick him, I felt a twinge of conscience, even pity. I stepped over him and left my cell.

Eighteen

The sheriff and his men found the remains of two more bodies, and their investigation turned up another 15 missing people. Although it had been a couple of months since I'd preyed on the mountain dwellers, the new findings alarmed the monks. The sheriff asked us to assemble so he could warn us to stay in after dark, when a culprit could lurk about with less danger of detection, and not to wander in the woods alone, even though no recent victims had been discovered.

That night I was taking some air at the edge of the woods, deliberating whether I should feed in the city or wait until the next night when the monks might be less alert. It was August, still warm, though I smelled rain in the heavy air and a breeze

V

stirred the branches. A circle of light suddenly glowed near the monastery and grew larger as it approached me.

"Who's out there?" Michael called when he heard me snap a limb. He scanned the trees with his flashlight.

The darkness that shielded me from him did not, of course, shield him from me. I watched his athletic form, dressed like me in jeans and a T-shirt, hike with determined strides toward the forest.

As he neared, he inadvertently shined the torturous light in my eyes.

"You're blinding me, for God's sake," I said.

"Brother Victor?" He lowered the light. "What are you doing here?"

"Taking a walk. My usual midnight stroll."

"I see. You're not afraid of the lunatic roaming the mountainside." His tone was lighter, more agreeable than it had ever been with me.

"I'll take my chances. Where are you going?"

"I'm worried about a couple of kids up there. Their father went to the city to find work. They're alone. He called from Knoxville just before compline. Said people were talking about the new bodies and he got worried. I told him I'd check in on his kids."

"I thought the bodies they found had been there for quite a while. The killer probably has disappeared now."

"Most likely. But he's worried all the same." Michael switched off the flashlight. His eyes had evidently grown accustomed to the darkness. He gazed at me in the meager light of the moon, his eyes bold but no longer full of loathing.

"Do you plan to stay up there with them?" I asked.

He shook his head. "No. Just to walk them to a house about half a mile from theirs so they can stay with someone. The man there's a big guy with a lot of guns."

"I'll go with you."

V

"It's quite a trek. Up by that radio tower." He pointed to the north, maybe three miles from the spot.

"Good exercise," I said.

We wound through the thicket, tree frogs and cicadas clamoring, probably in anticipation of the coming shower. Lightning seared the sky in the direction we were heading, followed by a crack of thunder.

"Looks like we'll be soaked," Michael said, stopping to catch his breath. Guided by the flashlight's beam, we'd been steadily climbing toward a footpath.

Once we reached the path the hiking was easier, though we continued to move up the incline, through heavy growth. Big drops of rain sifted through the branches and then poured from the sky. Even under the partial shelter of the foliage we got drenched. But Michael forged on, not the least bit hindered by the storm. His stride was big, his muscular arms steadily swinging. I thought he could wrestle his god if he wanted, like Jacob of the Hebrews.

It took an hour and a half to reach our destination, a shack nestled in the thicket, not far from the path. No lights glowed in the house. The screenless windows beneath the shaky roof of the porch were wide open.

"Watch your step," Michael said, whisking his light across gaps in the rotting planks of the porch. He hammered on the door with his fist.

The white face of a little girl appeared at the window.

"It's Brother Michael, Dora Anne," he said.

"Ginny, Brother Michael's here!" The girl disappeared from the window and the door swung open. She was 5 or 6, with a missing front tooth, limp blond hair, and a pale face splattered with freckles. She hugged Michael's legs excitedly.

"Brother Michael?" A girl of 16 or 17 appeared in a T-shirt

V

and cut-off jeans, folding her arms as though she were cold. Her short hair was tousled from sleeping. "What's a matter? Something wrong with Daddy?"

"No, no." Michael entered the cramped living room and I followed him. "He's just worried about you. He thinks you'd be safer staying with the Jacksons."

"They ain't found another body, have they?" Ginny said.

"I'm afraid so."

Ginny shivered and lit an oil lamp on a shelf. The pale light washed over a table with mismatched chairs, a sagging armchair, and two mattresses on the plywood floor, where water had puddled from our shoes. "Gives me the willies," she said. "We thought that crazy man done took off. Sheriff and his men been patrolling the woods."

"Did he cut off their heads?" Dora Anne looked up earnestly at Michael. "Ralph Jackson says he did. Then he stuck little needles into their body so they looked like porcupines."

"Ralph Jackson's just trying to scare you, Dora Anne. You just don't pay him any mind." Ginny turned to me, suspicion in her eyes. "You a brother too?"

"Yes. Brother Victor."

She nodded as though she had her doubts. "We'll be just fine, Brother Michael. Ain't no need to bother the Jacksons this time a night. I got Daddy's shotgun here and I can use it."

"How come you ain't never come up to see us before?" Dora Anne said to me.

"I'm new at the monastery." The little girl roused my appetite. Perhaps I would go down to the city to feed, I thought. If enough time remained.

"You wanna see a snake?" Dora said to me. "I got it in a jar."

"You can show him another time." Ginny grabbed Dora Anne's arm as she started toward the back door.

V

"Your father wants you to go to the Jacksons'," Brother Michael said to Ginny. "I think it's a good idea."

Ginny nodded. "Well, if you say so, Brother. Just hate to put 'em out. And Dora Anne ain't got nothing but flip-flops for walkin' in."

"I'll carry her," I said.

Michael looked at me with curiosity, as though I continued to surprise him by my benevolence.

"Yaaay! A piggyback ride!" Dora Anne jumped up and down, clapping her hands.

We waited until the rain slackened before heading for the Jacksons'. Dora Anne chattered the whole way, tugging at tree branches, squirming excitedly against my back, despite her sister's reprimands. Once we delivered them to the family, at nearly 2 in the morning, we tramped back to the monastery.

As I followed Michael, in answer to my question, he explained that many of the destitute mountain people chose to remain so far from civilization after the mines closed because of ignorance and fear of the city. And because of incestuous relationships they wanted to safeguard from the authorities. "I know one girl with three babies by her father," he said.

"Surely the sheriff must know about it?" Following Michael's lead, I stepped across a large puddle.

"He knows. But he also knows how life is here. The girl wouldn't leave her father if you paid her. And if they took her by force, she'd probably kill herself."

"That's a pity."

Michael reeled around. "You don't really mean that, do you?"

"No, I don't. Do you think it's a pity?"

Michael looked hard at me, despite the darkness. He could not make out my expression, but I could his, a gaze of recognition of an affinity between us. "There are worse things," he said and turned away.

V

We made the rest of the trek in silence, me savoring our new intimacy, Michael no doubt pondering it. We spoke only to warn each other of a treacherous limb or gully. But when we reached the fringe of the forest, where we could walk side by side, he spoke again.

"Thank you for being stern with Luke. I'm sorry if I misjudged you." He kept his eyes forward.

"And what if you didn't misjudge me?"

"Then you deserve even more credit for cutting him free."

I smiled in the darkness, though he had spoken quite seriously. "Have you talked to him? Is he still desperate?"

"He'll get over it. It's just infatuation."

"You sound as though you speak from experience."

Michael stopped. We were on the monastery property now. Our sneakers were sopping wet from the marshy ground. Michael steadied himself on my arm to remove his shoes. "It's no secret that monastic life attracts homosexuals. Men get to live with men, with impunity, with praise, at least from the Catholic world. I've had my share of attractions. Thanks." His eyes turned to mine when he straightened up and then darted away in discomfort.

"But you are dedicated to celibacy?" The opportunity seemed ripe for pressing him.

"I'm dedicated to God."

"And what does that mean, to be dedicated to God?"

"I discover it, day to day, like everybody else."

I grabbed Michael by the arm and stopped in my tracks, turning him toward me. "Let's stop playing games now, Michael. The intensity between us is as palpable as this flesh." I squeezed his firm arms. "You accused me of seducing Luke, but I wouldn't even attempt to seduce you, I desire you far too much for that. I can see you struggling, not against me but against yourself."

"Does this amuse you?"

V

"It gives me hope. May I hope?"

"Do you know why I struggle? It's not against my attraction to you. It's against the evil I find in my soul, the same evil I see reflected in your eyes. Both of us are proud, rebellious, but it's not just that. It's a coldness, like the ice trapping Satan at the bottom of Dante's inferno. A coldness that cuts us off from everyone."

"You've cared for Luke."

"I have a duty toward him. That's different."

"We're not sentimental types. Our hearts bother with nothing short of passion."

He continued gazing steadily into my eyes. I pulled him to me and kissed him. His full lips responded, his body pressed against mine. For a moment we merged with the loftiest mountain peak behind us, now star-crowned in the clearing skies.

"We can leave this place," I whispered in his ear as I embraced him.

He made no answer.

We kissed again in the dark entrance hall of the monastery and separated. My soul blazed for him. I longed for blood to calm myself, but dawn was too close now and I retreated to my cell. A figure sat wrapped in shadows outside the door.

"What are you doing here, Luke?" I nudged him with my foot to awaken him.

He shook off his sleep and got to his feet. "Where did y'all go?" he said accusingly.

"Go to bed." I opened my door and he followed me into the dark chamber.

"You was with Mike. I seen him going out to you."

He grabbed my arm. His eyes were filled with desperation.

I shook off his grip. "I said go to bed."

"No, Victor, you ain't gonna get away with this. No sir, you traitor. Both of you. You ain't gonna do this to me. Know what

V

I'll do?" He was nearly hysterical now, his voice trembling, his hands making fists at his sides. "I'll go to the abbot with everything. Hell, I'll confess everything about you and me. I'll tell him 'bout every time we fucked, every time you sucked my dick. You'll be outta here so fast you won't know what hit you."

I grabbed him by the shoulders. "Listen to me, boy. You'll keep your mouth shut or you'll be out of here too."

"No!" He tried to free himself from my grip. "I'll tell him, you bastard. You think I care what happens to me?"

I had no choice now. As Luke struggled in my hands, in the darkness of my cell, I plunged my fangs into his throat. For a moment, he melted into my arms, as though once again I were mounting him, and I felt his desire for me flare. But as I siphoned the warm, young blood, he collapsed, unconscious. I continued drinking until his heart, whose rhythm had moved from a frantic speed to the tempo of a solemn war drum, sounded a final beat.

Deep into the woods I carried his body, hiding it in the underbrush. I made it back to the monastery just as faint light rimmed the mountains. Quietly, I slipped into my tomb, as filled with dread as with the blood of my victim.

Michael Schiefelbein

V

The Beloved

Nineteen

Tolling, tolling, tolling. Throughout my fitful sleep in the close coffin, the bass voice of a bell, like an ancient prophet's lament, intruded into the dreams that followed my killing of Luke. When my nerves finally registered the sinking of the sun, my eyes flashed open in the dark chamber and I thought I heard the bell still. But silence prevailed. Around me the dusty skeletons lay, complacent, I thought, in their immobility, their finality. There were brief moments when I envied them.

The taste of Luke's blood was in my mouth. I thought I would retch. To kill a stranger, in the heat of lust for blood, in dire need of it, was like running a sword through an enemy during combat. No matter how young, how beautiful, how

V

brave the opponent, I plunged the sword up under the ribs as a matter of survival. But to kill a boy who fawned on me, though he hung like a stone around my neck, made me realize the darkness, the suffocating darkness of my life. The tight dimensions of the pine box, the close vault that held it, trapping awful shadows: How many times did I awake that night to see the chamber as a symbol of what I carried with me when, like a rodent, I crawled from its confines? But when upon my mind's screen were projected Michael's eyes, dark and intense, solemn and keen as a winter night's stormy sky, the darkness held hope, life that mocked the pious, insipid light of day.

I rose, eager to find Michael, stripping off my blood-splattered T-shirt and stuffing it under the mattress in my cell until I could bury it later. In a fresh habit, I ascended the stairs to the entry hall of the monastery. There, to my irritation, I found the sober-faced abbot awaiting me.

He greeted me with a nod. "Would you come into my office a moment, Brother Victor?"

I followed him, taking a seat in the leather chair across from his desk, where he seated himself. A pair of dim lamps glowed, leaving unbroken the shadows stretched across the books and high corners of the room.

"What is it, Brother Matthew?"

"Brother Luke has disappeared."

His unusual directness amused me. I imagined that, determined to overcome his intimidation of me, he had rehearsed this confrontation.

"He did not show up for lauds this morning, and when one of the brothers went to check on him, he found Luke's bed still made. We searched the greenhouse, the grounds, finally the whole monastery. There was no sign of him."

V

"You think he ran away?" I asked. I leaned back and crossed my legs.

"What do you think, Brother Victor?" The abbot removed his glasses and managed to look directly into my eyes.

"How should I know, Brother Matthew? After our conversation in the library I did exactly as I promised. I ended my association with Brother Luke."

"He made no attempt to keep up your friendship?"

"Of course he tried. As I told you, he was infatuated. But I insisted. Did he leave a note?" In the brief time I'd had to dispose of Luke's body there was no opportunity to scribble an explanation. Besides, I couldn't forge his hand, nor could I print something from a computer since he didn't have access to one and therefore couldn't have done that himself.

"No. Nothing. I hoped he might have said something to you about his whereabouts. I thought he must have run away out of anger or desperation, and that he might have warned you."

I shook my head. "I'm sorry. I know nothing."

Brother Matthew searched the wall behind me, his brow furrowed in distress, his delicate finger pressing his lips. Then he leveled his troubled gaze at me.

"Did you hear or see anything last night, any unusual noises inside the monastery, or outside? Did you go outside at all last night?"

I knew this was a test. Only in that second did I understand how little the abbot trusted me. "Yes, I took a walk. I know the sheriff told us to stay in, but I can't stay cooped up. I ran into Brother Michael. I'm surprised he didn't say anything to you. He was worried about some children left alone. I went up with him to take them to a safer place."

"Brother Michael did mention it." The abbot's eyes fell for a moment and then turned back on me after he'd composed himself. "I assembled the brothers, except for you, of course, because

V

it was daylight, to explain the situation and to ask if they heard or saw anything last night. Brother Michael told me you'd gone up the mountain and didn't see anything unusual. I just wondered if you had noticed anything before or after your trip."

"I see." I gazed at him until he lowered his eyes again. "No, I didn't notice anything. So you're concerned that Luke might have been attacked by the crazy man roaming the mountains?"

"It's a possibility we have to consider." He stood and went to the window. "Brother Luke took nothing with him, as far as we can tell. He had no means of transportation. To hitchhike into town in the middle of the night, on a country road…well, that seems pretty unlikely. At least the sheriff thinks so. He's had men searching the road into Knoxville all day."

"Are they searching the woods too?"

The abbot turned and rested his hands on the back of his chair. "Yes. If Luke did wander into the woods. Well, just pray for him, Brother."

I nodded.

"Sheriff Johnson will be here shortly to question you. He's already spoken to the others."

"I don't see that I can help him."

"Still, he wants to cover all the bases."

When the sheriff arrived, the abbot left us alone in his office. The stocky, 50ish man sat on the edge of a wing-back chair and, resting his elbows on his knees, wrote my responses on a page in a clipboard. He looked exhausted, straining to see his own notes through his bifocals. He wore a khaki uniform with short sleeves and two buttons open at the neck in the heat. His reddish beard needed trimming.

"Now, Brother," he drawled, glancing up at me with steady gray eyes. "You say you was outside last night till what time?"

"Nearly dawn. It took us that long to get back from the

V

Jacksons' house. Didn't Brother Michael tell you all this?" I made little attempt to hide my impatience.

"All a formality, Brother. Bear with me here." He jotted down something. "And you saw or heard nothing suspicious?"

"It was raining. We were talking. I didn't notice anything."

"Mmm-hmm." He scribbled again.

"You think there was foul play?"

"Too early to know." He straightened up to yawn, sat back in the chair, and crossed his legs as though we were having a very amiable conversation. "You and Brother Luke was pretty close, I hear." He removed his bifocals and put them in his shirt pocket.

"You could say that, I suppose." I stared steadily at him.

"You suppose? Were y'all on the outs?" He tapped his pen against a gold cap on a bottom tooth as he peered at me with interest.

"Luke was making a pest of himself. He followed me around like a dog. I told him to find another hero. I'm sure the abbot told you he advised me to talk to Luke. He probably also told you Luke was upset with me. Which explains why he ran away."

"If he did run away."

"Yes."

"You don't seem too bent out of shape about Brother Luke. I guess it's probably good to keep a level head when there's nothing you can do." He continued to eye me with interest.

"Exactly. If there is something I can do—"

"Well, in fact there is one thing you might help me with. You mind if I take a peek at your bedroom? Abbot said it was down in the cellar under the church."

"Yes. I have a skin condition. I can't take any amount of sunlight. Why do you want to see my cell?" Civility had never come natural to me, and I made little effort to hide my resentment now.

"Oh, just a formality. You know. Got to poke around the whole place."

V

The sheriff followed me down the dark stairs. When we got to the crypt he stopped to examine the tablets on the walls.

"Well, look at that. This 'un died pert near 100 years ago." He had put on his glasses to read the dates on the middle tablet. "I guess the one down here's the newest dearly departed." He advanced toward my tomb.

"Yes." I stepped forward. "Do you mind if we get this inspection over? I have some work to do."

"'Course, Brother. 'Course. Lead on."

He looked around my cell, under the bed, under the desk. "You mind?" He pointed to the dresser and opened each drawer.

He approached the bed again and my heart stirred. Under the mattress lay the bloody T-shirt. Boring into his mind with my glance, I willed him away from it. He stopped in his tracks, scratched his head as though he'd forgotten what he was doing, and glanced at his clipboard. "Well, that'll do her," he said.

After nosing around in the boiler room and the storage areas, he departed.

Compline was already over, and the monks had retired. I grabbed the bloody T-shirt and tossed it into my tomb. I went out into the night for air, but the humid atmosphere weighed me down as if the ocean itself pressed me to its depths.

Michael Schiefelbein

Twenty

After 2,000 years, I found mystery in few things. But Michael proved to be an enigma. After feeling our eyes, our souls connect, speaking without words as we traipsed through the woods, as we crossed the grounds behind the monastery the night I sucked the life from Luke, I expected to see him nightly, to hold secret rendezvous of sweet passion, to lead him away from St. Thomas, ultimately to the Kingdom of Darkness. But I walked the grounds, the woods, alone for more than a week. I saw no sign of him under the September moon.

In chapel he gazed steadily from his breviary to the high altar, as though he conducted telepathic communications with one of the plaster saints in the niches. He knelt when the others

V

knelt, but not meekly with his head bowed. Even as he knelt, his keen eyes bore into some private apparition. I frequently drew his gaze to me with my own bold stare, and for many seconds we would survey one another as though we placidly watched our reflections in a mirror. But he did not linger after prayers, and I did not pursue him.

Until finally I noticed a change in his expression. His contemplation of me across the aisle warmed to desire, and I felt in an instant how much he craved me. That night I found him in the greenhouse, dark except for a lone bulb in the far corner. Outside, branches brushed wistfully against the glass roof. Passing tables of ivy twisting down to the slate floor and row upon row of bright annuals, I found Michael bent over a cart of herbs divided into small white cartons. He wore gym trunks and a tank top. His shoulders and arms were brown from the sun, his hair gathered into a ponytail. He glanced up as I approached, and then continued removing the herbs from their containers and inserting them into trays of dirt.

"You haven't come to me," I said. Humidifiers made the air practically unbearable even though I had changed out of my habit after the sheriff left and slipped into light clothing.

"I needed time." With a small trowel, he loosened a sprig of parsley from its container and planted it in the earth.

"Time? For what? To confirm my desire for you or yours for me?"

"Neither." He glanced up as he continued transplanting the herbs. "A very wise woman once taught me to wait, to listen."

"Listen? To what? To God?" I folded my arms.

"To the night, to the wind, to my fantasies, my nightmares. To spirits, too." He looked up again.

"And what kind of spirits speak to you?" I wasn't sure if he was playing with me.

Michael Schiefelbein

V

"All kinds. Evil. Good. Spirits of ages past. Spirits speaking through the pages of books. The old woman, Jana, was my grandmother, my mother's mother, a Creole in New Orleans, where I grew up. She ran a tarot shop in the French Quarter, voodoo dolls on the walls, and crucifixes, altars for saints, candles burning everywhere. She had quite a clientele. Sometimes I sat in the corner while she read their tarot cards."

"Your grandmother raised you?"

"No. My father. A thick-headed Italian drunk. My mother died when I was a baby. But I spoke to her, through Jana. She burned spices at her mausoleum in St. Louis Cemetery."

"You are serious."

He looked up as though surprised I had doubted.

"Come walk with me, in the woods. Tell me about this sorceress grandmother of yours."

"Let me finish these first. I'll meet you on the grounds in half an hour."

Thirty minutes later, he strode up the incline from the buildings, cutting a confident, athletic silhouette in the moonlight. I led the way to a familiar path. When we reached it, I turned to him.

"Not a stickler about the Grand Silence, are you?"

"The Sabbath is made for man, not man for the Sabbath." He stooped to inspect a glittering stone, then hurled it into the trees.

"Tell me more about your adventures in spiritualism." I longed to take him in my arms, but his reserve stopped me.

He shrugged. "What's to tell? I spoke to my mother. I've done it more than once. I've spoken to Jana too, now that she's gone. I learned quite a bit from her."

"Such as?"

"Such as discerning forces at work around me, attuning myself to them." He spoke as though he referred to a power no

V

more unusual than the ability to tell whether the moon was full.

"Forces? You mean evil spirits or some such thing?"

He looked at me with curiosity. "Evil and good."

"Not a very monklike thing, is it? Why enter a monastery if you want to tell fortunes in the French Quarter?"

"Why did I enter? I don't want to bore you with all of that."

I grabbed his arm. "You know nothing you could say would bore me."

"Yes, I know."

"Then tell me."

We had steadily climbed the hillside to the clearing where Luke and I used to come, about 100 meters from where I had disposed of his body. Michael's eyes had adjusted to the dark, and during our walk he'd turned off the flashlight he carried. But now he turned it back on and scanned the clearing.

"What are you looking for?"

"Just a place to sit. Over there." He pointed to the fallen tree.

We sat on the dew-dampened ground, leaning against the tree. Michael folded his legs yoga-style and leaned his head back to view the stars.

"This is my fifth year in these mountains," he said. "The life of a monk has fascinated me since childhood. The ritual, the silence, the solitude. Working with the earth. Poring through volumes on philosophy and mysticism. The sublime chants."

"And celibacy?"

"As a discipline, it has its place. It strengthens the soul."

"For what purpose? To overcome evil, I suppose."

He smiled at my cynical tone. "Wasn't it idealism that brought you to the monastery?"

"No. It was anger. Survival, too, and power."

He registered the passion in my words but made no response, only turning his eyes back to the sky. "I used to think

V

I had to fight evil. But Jana corrected me. Evil, she said, lurks everywhere, even in your own soul—especially there. Never underestimate it. Don't pretend to banish it. Respect it. Listen to it, and even evil will speak to you."

"Don't tell me you have a closet full of voodoo dolls."

Michael laughed and slapped my leg.

I grasped his hand, shoved him gently to the ground, and, lying over him, kissed him. The heat of desire flashed through my veins. His heart pounded too, through his meaty chest. I felt him stiffen against my loins. So much blood, so close to my thirsty soul, pumping so mightily, like the raging waters behind a dam.

"No, not now," he said.

"I want you."

"Not now!" He pushed me off him.

I was furious. I wanted to shout, *Do you know who I am?* The words echoed through my head, discipline alone restraining my tongue from speaking them.

But Michael's eyes told me he knew what I was thinking anyway. And his unspoken response, as clear and firm as his own voice, sounded in my brain: "The link between body and soul—it confuses me, Victor. I'm learning."

Twenty-one

Autumn came and vanished, the oak tree in the courtyard surrendering its last leaves in mid-November when, by day, I knew,
the sky grew ashen and more intrusive through the naked
branches of the woods. With the passing months fire raged
through my veins and my spirit marched toward the trophy I'd
coveted for two millennia: life with an eternal comrade.

I met Michael every night, and while the others wasted their
hours in mortal sleep, we trod the woods under skies moonlit or
black. We discussed occult and mystical volumes in the shadows of the
library's stacks, and embraced in the humid jungle of the greenhouse.

Yet both of us guarded our secrets: I, my predatory and preternatural nature; he, the reason for his caution, his reluctance

V

to yield his body to me despite the passion he could not hide.

I longed to take him, wholly, lustfully, his soul along with his body. But a companion worthy of me must surrender freely. His strength, his mysterious mind, raised him higher and higher in my estimation. Still, as the energy between our souls intensified like the friction of pistons in an engine, my restraint threatened to explode.

In the meantime, after our nocturnal rendezvous, I continued to feed on undesirables in the city—prostitutes, vagrants, drug addicts holed up in condemned shacks. Driven by my desire for Michael, I tore at jugulars with a fury, lapped up warm blood from full breasts, sated myself to the point of drunkenness on a slew of victims in one night. The headlines of the newspaper flashed my rampages to the whole city—terrified though I had restricted my prey to undesirables. The police had established that the murders took place between midnight and dawn. They kept surveillance not only in the red light district and the projects, but in the other urban neighborhoods, where half their fleet of cars patrolled the streets through the night.

The vast number of murders brought in federal agents to investigate—not only the killings in the city, but those in the mountains too. The whole cursed area, yet again in my long life, became the notorious central subject of the local and also wider-ranging media. I knew as technology advanced investigators could easily trace my path of destruction across the globe. It was only a matter of time before they linked the blood feasts in Knoxville with those in the English village I'd escaped.

A group of monks gathered around the television one night to watch a national report on the massacres.

The expressionless newscaster, unnaturally tan, peered into the camera. "Federal agents still search for leads in what has now become an international crime. Scotland Yard believes a cult could be at work in the killings, most of which involved the draining of the victim's blood, usually through the jugular vein, vampire-style. In fact, U.S. investigators believe a satanic cult steeped in vampire lore is behind the massacres. We interviewed FBI Director Walter Searling today in Washington."

Here the camera flashed to a hallway in the FBI building. A lanky blond reporter held a microphone in front of the neat, mustachioed director.

"We have followed the pattern of killings," he said, "and we're certain that a series of murders in Boyshire, England, were committed by the same group as those in Knoxville. We've been working closely with Scotland Yard, and we are certain we will find the perpetrators."

"So you're certain that a group of people are responsible for the crimes?" The reporter took the microphone away from the director's lips just long enough to ask her question.

"No, we are not, although it would be more feasible considering the widespread nature of the killings. We might be trailing someone like the Boston Strangler or Jack the Ripper, but psychologists tell us that serial killers usually restrict themselves to specific geographical areas."

"What about Ted Bundy?"

"There are always exceptions. We're considering the possibility that one person is acting alone, but it's most likely a group."

"Any clues at all about the identity of the killer or killers?"

"We're putting together a profile of the perpetrators. It's just a matter of time. In the meantime, local police have increased surveillance in the Knoxville area."

Following the interview several residents of Knoxville recounted to another reporter the grisly scenes I'd left behind. The brothers leaned forward on their chairs or shook their heads.

"What a god-awful thing." Brother Raymond took a drink from a bottle of beer and wiped his lips.

V

"They shouldn't show this gruesome stuff on television." Brother Herbert, a big-jowled professor on sabbatical from a university in Europe, frowned as the camera panned across a bloody bed.

The others sighed and moaned, and for the rest of the social hour the killings formed the topic of conversations around the coffee table and the bar. Michael had watched the news program intensely, but I saw nothing in his expression suggesting he suspected the truth.

How long, I wondered, until the investigators found monasteries at the center of both massacres? How long before they came to hunt me down in the crypt of St. Thomas?

The moment was ripe for claiming a place in the Dark Kingdom. Once I'd secured my consort, I could leave the detestable life of feedings and tombs and flights from those who hunted me.

The silence of Joshu over the summer and autumn months went unbroken, a sign that I had finally found his replacement. But though no visions of Joshu visited me, other apparitions did. Often, as I slumbered in the dank mausoleum, Tiresia's eyes, full of malice and sensuality, teased me in my dreams. "What are you waiting for, Victor?" she would say. "Your world awaits you. The time has come." Her ebony limbs and breasts cut a silhouette into a full white moon. A sleek mare galloped across the sky and Tiresia's creator and consort, a barrel-chested, hairy soldier, dismounted and wrapped her in his embrace.

Horrible apparitions haunted me too, apparitions of Luke. As I slept in the coffin or became entranced by a demonic book, he would moan and call my name from the woods. His voice would come closer and closer and finally he would stand naked before me, the gash in his throat oozing blood that streamed down his pallid chest. His listless eyes

V

would fall on me and, panting for air, he would speak:

"Let me be your consort, Victor. Take me from this hell."

"What hell?" I would demand.

"It's cold here. Like ice, Victor, like ice. I'm freezing." He would futilely rub his arms. "Take me up."

"You've passed to another world. It's too late. Go back, damn you."

During the vision I would will Luke to vanish, the way the dreamer tries to alter a nightmare just as the demon's hand reaches for him, but my mind had no effect. Plaintive Luke remained, gasping for air, repeating his speech, until I reached out to kill him once again, when he would bare his teeth at me and fade into nothing.

Michael, on the other hand, appeared to enjoy more comforting visits from the supernatural world. When he'd first told me of Jana and his dabblings in spiritualism, I was amused. Not that I doubted the communications he received: Every human has a sixth sense, as they say, though in most it goes undiscovered or ignored. However, the magnitude of his experiences and the identity of his visitor roused my interest and envy.

The first time I witnessed his ecstatic seizure was a December night during Advent, when purple cloths draped the altar and pulpit. When Michael failed to show up in the crypt at the appointed hour, I searched for him and found him in the dark chapel, kneeling before the crucifix on the high altar, completely naked, his hands stretched out as though he were crucified. Light from the vigil lamp suspended by a chain near the tabernacle cast a red glow across his face.

"Michael, what are you doing?"

I touched his shoulder but he gave no sign of recognizing me. His eyes, like the eyes of a corpse, stared ahead as though they focused on nothing at all. His body was as cold as a corpse,

V

too. Giving up my attempt to shake him from this reverie, I sat on the sanctuary steps to observe him and, if I could, to enter into his strange communion with the world beyond.

For a quarter of an hour his muscular arms stayed frozen in place, his body as immobile as the statues above him. Then, as though riding a mighty jet of air, he rose, locked into the same position, until he was level with the crucifix mounted on the gabled apex of the reredos.

Then he chanted over and over "O Crux, ave spes unica," words from a hymn I particularly despised—the damned "placing hope in the cross." His clear voice reached a crescendo and then faded. Finally he struck his breast and muttered, "Eripe me, Domine, ab homine malo." *Who was the evil man he sought refuge from?* I wondered. *I who could give him what heaven only pretended to give?*

Suddenly the pallor of the marble corpus of the crucifix melted away like a coat of paint, revealing the brown flesh, the true features of Joshu himself.

"Joshu!" I yelled, jumping to my feet. Levitating myself to the pair floating near the vaulted ceiling, I tried to grasp first Joshu, then Michael, but what seemed to be a wall of glass prevented me from making contact. I remained a spectator.

Now Michael's body relaxed and spun around toward me. His cock was erect. He licked his lips and sensuously caressed his chest. Joshu approached him and, flinging his arms around his waist, kissed his neck. In that moment I thought I beheld twin Joshus, their sinewy bodies, their strong features and dark coloring were so alike. Michael panted, Joshu's hands remaining fixed around him, and he finally moaned as though climaxing. But though his cock remained stiffened by the blood of passion, nothing spewed forth at the moment of orgasm.

Joshu released him and resumed his place on the reredos.

V

"No, Joshu!" I cried. "Come back, damn you!"

His placid face showed no sign of hearing my demand. The human color faded from his flesh and he solidified once again into the corpus that resembled a pious artist's fantasy, not the man who smelled of Hebrew wine and spices, of labor's musky sweat, of the desert and the sea.

Michael floated back to the sanctuary and landed in a heap near his crumpled habit. Descending to him, I crouched to touch his forehead, before like ice, now burning with fever. Unconscious and trembling, he moaned and called out Joshu's name. I scooped his naked body in my arms, along with his clothes, and carried him to his cell by way of the corridor along the library, a safer route than past the abbot's rooms. I lay him upon his narrow bed and, checking the dark corridor before closing the door, rinsed a washcloth with cool water from the basin in the corner and mopped his face and neck.

For more than an hour I sat next to his bed in the darkness, bathing his flesh, until finally the fever broke and his limbs calmed. Color filled his wan face again, as it had the marble cheeks of Joshu's corpus, and he breathed quietly in a sound sleep. Near dawn, while I sat lost in thought, his eyes opened and he turned his face toward me.

"Victor? Is that you?"

I leaned over and touched his cheek.

"Did I…was there an apparition? Where did you find me?"

"In the chapel. Raving like a lunatic. Do you remember what you saw?"

He shook his head and kissed my hand.

"What do the others think of your raptures?"

"No one knows. Not now. Luke did. He found me a couple of times, outside, near the woods. I told him it was epilepsy."

"Maybe it is."

V

"You know it's not. You know." He gazed at me admiringly.

"Victor…" He brushed my arm with his lips.

I crawled into the bed next to him and found his lips, heated now but not with fever. His kiss stirred my desire for him, the desire I'd struggled to restrain until his will moved, until now, when its motion surged like a flooded stream. I stripped off my clothes and into that stream cast my soul, taking him in my arms, kissing his neck, his chest, taking in my mouth his engorged cock as though I were a hungry infant at the breast.

When he moaned in pleasure, his chest rising and falling, not with the regularity I had seen in the weight room but with urgency and a quickening, erratic rhythm, with an abandonment of predictability and control, I entered him. The warm passage expanded without a hint of resistance, as though my full cock belonged there, wrapped in the warm, bloody membrane. I drilled into that blood, pumped seconds ago from the excited heart of my beloved. I felt the blood there, and smelled blood on his lips. I felt blood coursing through his every vein and artery, bearing in its red tide his very soul—to me, to me. I longed for the blood, longed to drink of that soul. My fangs, now extended to their full length, sought it, but as the spasms of consummation shook his sweaty body, I turned my head away. He must be my lover, not my victim.

VI
The Proposal

Twenty-two

On Christmas, fresh snow piled three inches on the branches and drifted against the stone walls on the east side of St. Thomas. Irrationally or not, I breathed more easily, thinking that by shrouding the ground, the snow would trap the ghost of Luke, who continued to haunt me. But it was no use. As dried as it now was, I could smell Luke's blood on the shirt I'd deposited in my tomb. Destroying it or burying it in the woods was out of the question now that federal agents were searching the area with renewed vigor. News reports only speculated as to why the agents had returned to the woods above the monastery, since the director would reveal nothing about the agency's motives. I knew it was because they needed Luke's body to link the crimes to St.

V

Thomas. Even someone without my keen perceptions would sense the sheriff had suspected me, and the drill I was subjected to by one of the agents only confirmed this impression.

"Now, Brother Victor," he said, sitting behind the abbot's desk with a pad and an expensive fountain pen. "How would you classify your relationship with Brother Luke?" His arrogant manner heightened his attractiveness. He had a boyish face but a stocky, well-built frame. His collar fit tight around his thick neck.

"I've been over this with the sheriff." I stared straight into his eyes, but he betrayed no intimidation.

"Formality, Brother. When we need to go over the same ground, we do. Right now, I need for you to answer me."

"We were friends." I crossed my legs and tried to keep myself calm. "He was young, looking for a mentor. I was the mentor."

"Just a mentor?"

"What are you asking?"

"Are you a homosexual, Brother?" His eyes remained leveled with mine. The agency had chosen well when they hired this cold, direct official.

"No."

"I've heard different."

"So? It's not true. I'm a monk. Celibate, Mr. Andrews. What kind of a monastery do you think we have here?"

He recapped his fountain pen. "That's the exact question we're working on, Brother. When we piece it together, you'll be the first to know."

I left him in the office when he'd finished his interrogation. Which of the monks had reported my unnatural liaison with Luke, I wondered. The pathetic abbot? One of the head-in-the-clouds scholars who'd for once noticed something outside his own esoteric world? It didn't matter. Even if I did covet my monastic refuge, I never sought to please my foolish companions.

V

No witch-hunts would be held within the sacred walls now anyway, no matter who in the monastery observed my movements. Creating a scandal in the world without could injure the reputation of the order, could result in the abbot's demotion. Perhaps the arrogant agent himself had surmised the truth. So be it. My time was coming.

A freak blizzard stopped the FBI's search for a whole day. That night, the wind howling in my ears, I sped through the air to the spot where I'd buried Luke's remains. A downed tree sank into the ravine where I'd dug a grave with one hand while I lifted the trunk with the other. Snow filled the entire ditch and camouflaged even the tree itself beneath a drift.

I'd no choice now. If the agents discovered Luke's remains, I'd have to flee, and flee without Michael. The time was close. Between us, close as the dawn, lay the pact, itself a dawn whose bright rays even I could bask in.

The icy flakes coated my brows, my hair by now. The cold stung my hands as I clawed beneath the tree, which I'd shifted with some difficulty, laden as it was with snow. Blinking in the storm, I kept an eye out for ambitious FBI interlopers while my hand groped for the remnants of my prey. I felt a shock of brittle hair, then pulled up Luke's skull, skinless now after all these months, and dropped it into the garbage bag I'd brought with me. His habit, his loose bones, his shoes came next, all embedded in the frozen earth, which seemed to tighten its grip the more I dug and pulled. But at last I had every scrap of him. I replaced the tree, scooped snow back into the ravine, and, pitting myself against the storm, flew back to the monastery.

Nightmares or not, the skeleton could be concealed in only one place: the mausoleum. The stream was frozen and would be dragged when it thawed—soon, given the usually mild Tennessee winters. Transporting the bones to another location,

V

to a farm or beyond the city, involved the risk of being seen. Besides, I believed the key to conquering my nightmares was to face the ghost who haunted me. What had I to fear from a cluster of bones, I who had slept in the midst of bones for 2,000 years?

I trod quietly through the dark entryway with my treasure and stole down the stone stairs to the crypt. The mausoleum's gate whined as I opened it. I ducked into the tomb and jerked the lid from one of the vaults. On the neat skeleton of a monk, clad in the tatters of his habit, I dumped the new, jumbled bones and the habit and shoes of a youth who, if not for his idiocy, would still live.

When day arrived I slept like a baby.

Twenty-three

Twice more I witnessed Michael's strange seizures. The first time, he repeated his conference with the transformed marble corpus of Joshu, chanting the same hymn, muttering the same Latin injunction about an evil man. Again I carried him to his cell and we made passionate love. The second fit overcame him in the woods in early February, after the agents had given up their futile search for Luke's remains. The snow had long ago melted. In the prematurely balmy air we were hiking along the path through the woods when Michael launched into a sprint. At first I thought he was playing.

"Just try to get away!" I called after him.

Waiting until he had disappeared beyond a slope, I flew at

V

the speed of my thoughts, arriving at a place where the path divided, part of it disappearing into the trees and winding around an abandoned shack. After standing against an oak for a good time, I called to him.

"Is this a challenge? All right then, I accept." I laughed, believing he hid from me in the woods.

But as I tramped up the hill, a light caught my eye, fire blazing through the trees. I found him, a glimmering cloak draped around his naked shoulders, his eyes raised to a limb where an old woman rested. A turban like the headdresses worn by American slaves wrapped her small, dark head. A large, bold print splashed her robe with purple and green, visible to me despite the darkness.

"This is Jana, Victor." Michael threw his arm around me.

His eyes were glazed, as though he spoke in his sleep.

"Yes." I studied the shriveled hag.

"We meet at last, good Victor," she said. "The World of Darkness bids you greetings." She spoke with a heavy accent—Creole, I assumed. Her eyes were full of mischief.

"The Dark Kingdom? You reside there?"

"I reside nowhere. I flit about in the darkness."

"What kind of apparition are you?" I asked, doubtful.

"One conjured by this one." She glanced at Michael, who continued looking on in a daze.

"Ah, only a shadow then," I said.

"A projection of the shadow within Michael's own soul. He would know evil."

"For what purpose?"

"To reckon with it, to understand its power."

I laughed. "Understand it? Vanish, hag, there's nothing you can teach."

Her eyes returned to Michael. "Witness the power of evil, boy."

V

She faded to a transparent image and then vanished altogether.

Michael collapsed. The cloak had disappeared along with the apparition, leaving him naked. His body could have been a corpse, it was so cold. I dressed him and lay with him near the fallen tree until he opened his eyes and inhaled deeply the balmy air, spiced with the clean scent of firs.

"It's very dark, Victor."

"Yes." I stroked his hair. "I've learned to love the night. With my illness, I have no choice. Do you remember your apparition?"

He shook his head. "Something sad. That's all I know."

After he regained his sense of orientation, we relaxed together against the fallen tree, and I asked him about his mystical experiences.

He stared thoughtfully toward the stars. "I'm not sure what to say. I've had them ever since I can remember. I know when they come. I wake up naked and confused. Sometimes I remember the content exactly. Sometimes it's just a feeling of doom or lightness, depending."

"What about this time?" I said, grasping his hand. "What did you feel?"

He shrugged. "Fear."

"Of what?"

"I don't know. Who can make sense of dreams?"

"But you take these spells to heart." I paused. "Do you fear me?"

"You asked me that before. In the weight room. Should I fear you, Victor?"

"No, I would never harm you. In fact, what I want…"

I turned my head to consider whether the moment was ripe for opening the door, at least an inch. "What I want is to give you something."

"What?" His dark eyes gazed at me intensely.

I released his hand and got up. I paced for a few moments

V

with my hands behind my back and then I faced him. He had drawn up his legs to hug his knees.

"I want you to think of an image."

"An image?"

"Anything, a broom, a car, anything. Only focus on it as though you were projecting it on a screen in your mind. Go ahead."

Michael closed his eyes. Within seconds of concentrating on his thoughts, the image of a skull reproduced itself in my mind.

"Why a skull?" I demanded.

"You see it?" Michael opened his eyes in surprise.

"No." I sat down next to him. "Close your eyes again. Imagine the skull. That's right. Now watch." I once again directed my will to Michael's mind, where blood now streamed from the skull's eyes. "See the blood?"

"Yes."

"Keep focused on it. Move toward it. Do you feel it?"

His breathing grew more rapid. "Yes," he said, excitedly.

"Feel it. Feel the power, the strength. Feel the lust, the hunger."

"Yes."

I shook him at the height of his pleasure and he opened his eyes, still panting.

"I want to give you this passion as often as you want."

The pleasure vanished from his face and he glared at me in indignation. "How is it yours to give, Victor?"

"I can't tell you now."

"You can't tell me?" He jerked his hand away from me and stood. "You ask me about intimate visions, but you can't tell me how you get inside my head?"

I climbed to my feet and faced him. "Don't push me. Strong chains are forged slowly. Like the bond between us."

"You think I withhold secrets from you?"

"You've no reason to." I grabbed his arm when he shook his

V

head in exasperation and started to walk away. "Wait, please. I have a long past, Michael. You've got to let me unfold it slowly. You've got to trust me. You're the one who believes in waiting, remember?"

He gazed steadily into my eyes as though he were trying to read my thoughts. Then he relaxed in resignation. "All right, Victor. I'll leave it to you."

He remained true to his word, his discipline taking over when his pride reared its head, no small feat since his ego matched my own. It was my own impatience that worried me. I burned for our consummation; had I followed my impulses, I would have revealed everything in an instant, but at the risk of taxing even Michael's courage to hear the truth. A gradual disclosure alone would ensure our future.

One night in the library's reading room, as we pored over so-called "apocryphal" volumes on the life of Joshu, Michael went to retrieve another book from the stacks. When he arrived at the fifth level, reached only by the flights of narrow stairs he'd climbed, I was waiting for him there, having willed myself to the spot. His gaze absorbed the significance of the accomplishment, but without a word he walked to the shelves for his book.

At other times I heaved a fallen tree from the forest path or crushed a stone into powder. In the refectory one night, I caught his eye during the reading and made a sign for him to watch while my eyes seared into the mind of fat Brother Athanasius as he read from the Lives of the Saints. Suddenly confused, Athanasius stopped and returned to the beginning of the passage. After he stopped and started twice more at my prompting, the abbot motioned for him to take a seat.

Michael registered my powers with gravity, but stayed true to his promise, demanding no explanation.

One night during Lent I decided to broach the subject of the Kingdom of Darkness. Michael had spent the day spreading

V

mulch around trees on the property and we inspected the hedges near the buildings to determine how much more was needed. When we returned to my cell, he sprawled out on the bed, exhausted. I straddled the desk chair, facing him. The tired lines around his eyes showed up even in the soft lamplight. We chatted awhile about trivial matters, and after a long pause in the conversation I spoke.

"What do you think heaven is like?"

"It's 3 in the morning, Victor. I'm not in the mood for a catechism lesson."

"This isn't catechism."

The seriousness of my tone got his attention. He rolled over and propped his head on his hand. "Go on."

"I think people are goaded toward it by some strange lofty ideas. Blessed union with the creator. Eternal blessedness. What is that?"

"What happens in eternity is anybody's guess."

"Guessing's not the problem. It's spelled out by Scriptures. The Book of Revelation paints a nice picture—the masses kneeling at the throne of God, singing, praising. For eternity. Frozen forever on their knees. Sounds like hell to me."

"What about Dante? Paradise is contemplating God, according to him."

"Contemplation be damned. We're made for action, life, movement, pleasure." I pounded the back of the chair with my fist.

"From the way Dante describes hell, I don't think we'll find much pleasure there." He yawned.

"What if there were another option, Michael?" I got up and sat next to him on the bed, my elbows on my knees. "What if you could spend eternity laughing, making love, feasting, living like a god yourself?"

He rolled onto his back and clasped his hands behind his

Michael Schiefelbein

V

head. "That's what Lucifer was after, if I remember the story."

I shook my head. "Lucifer wanted to rule the same damned heaven. He lost the war, that's all."

"What are you saying? A third realm exists? We've all been brainwashed into being good so we can go to heaven?"

"It's true. The Dark Kingdom is a place for the elect, bold souls. A realm of gods." I paused. "It's the source of my powers. I can give you a glimpse of it."

The adrenaline pumped through him now. His eyes were keen, every nerve of his body ready to receive. But I had said enough for the time being.

"Stay patient," I said. "I'll show you everything soon." I kissed him good night and asked him to leave, despite his curiosity.

How did I know I could enter the Kingdom of Darkness? It was like an animal's instinct to mate, latent until the right moment, when it flared into the single impulse of its existence. My movements in the night, despite centuries of my own ignorance, had not been directionless, I now sensed. My mating dance had begun—the time to carry my prospective consort across the boundary of darkness for a taste of what awaited him once he served his term as a nocturnal predator.

After he left I rushed so rapidly through the night that my cheeks stung and my ears rang when I lighted on a dark Knoxville street to feed. Ravenous, I forced myself to move with caution since the police still patrolled the streets. Sweet, rich blood hung in the March air, so much that for a moment I felt disoriented, as though pulled in a hundred directions. "Focus, focus," I urged myself, and when I obeyed my own command the route to take traced itself in my mind, as vivid and red as the blood I sought.

A porch wrapped around a modest frame house, meticulously painted and adorned with shutters and lacy trim along

V

the gable. I scanned the rest of the houses in the quiet cul-de-sac. Every window was dark. Still, to play it safe, I walked around back and through the gate of a picket fence. A decal on the back door announced "Proud to Be a Vietnam Vet" over an unfurled American flag. I pulled the knob of the locked door slowly and as quietly as possible until the bolt tore through the door frame.

The snug kitchen smelled of bay leaves. In the living room, afghans draped sagging armchairs. From a photo above the antiquated television gazed a shiny-faced young man in a dress Marine jacket and white cap. The boards squeaked under my step as I followed a scent down a hallway. I paused, listened. Someone turned in a bed and sighed.

The first door I came to was slightly ajar. I crept in toward a large four-poster bed in the center of the room, where I could discern a woman's weathered face. Snatching her robe from the foot of the bed, I pressed it over her mouth. Her eyes opened; she struggled and moaned; her flailing arm knocked a glass to the floor.

"Mama! You all right?" The man's voice came from the adjacent room.

I twisted the old woman's neck until it snapped, and hid behind the door as the hall light came on.

"You OK, Mama?"

When no response came from the bed, a man in a wheelchair rolled into the room, his long ponytail jiggling as he worked the wheels. "Mama?"

Before he could discover my deed, I grabbed his shoulders and plunged my fangs into his bearded throat. He clutched my hair as blood spurted from his jugular until he lost consciousness. I drank greedily for almost ten minutes, emptying every vein of his tobacco-laced blood.

After feeding, I surveyed the scene before me: one body slumped over in the wheelchair, the other still staring toward the

Michael Schiefelbein

V

door, arms stretched out like a cross. "Soon, now," I said to myself. "Soon I will stop creeping in the night, desperate for prey."

I sped back to the edge of the woods and walked across the grounds to the monastery. As I came around to the front of the building, I caught a glimpse of a white car disappearing down the drive without its lights. I was sure it stopped behind a cluster of trees, but with dawn only half an hour away I couldn't investigate.

My sleep was fitful. I dreamed that blood gushed again from my victim's throat, but every time I stooped to drink from the red jet, it ceased. When I sucked the musty, hairy throat, it yielded nothing. Thirst maddened me. I stalked victim after victim, but each time I caught my prey it turned into a half-familiar corpse I had drained long ago.

The scene changed then. A golden throne rose from the midst of four six-winged creatures bulging with eyes in front and back. In the throne glowed a translucent figure whose crown of jasper and carnelian seemed an extension of the throne itself. The ruler lifted a scroll, the creatures fell to their knees, a man approached. In a white robe, his skin now alabaster, his hair like bleached fleece, the man accepted the scroll.

"Joshu!" I screamed from the midst of a throng of people. But he did not hear.

"Worthy is the lamb that was slain!" The crowd chanted.

"Damn you, Joshu!" I screamed, immobilized by the bodies pressing around me. "Damn you then! Rehearse your coronation for eternity. I will live!"

Twenty-four

The night after I'd preyed on the crippled man, Michael approached me after vespers and said to meet him in the weight room during the recreation period. When I asked why it couldn't wait until our usual meeting time in my cell he shook his head gravely and whispered, "We can't. I'll explain."

"Shut the door," he said, straining to lift a bar loaded with weights.

"They'll be suspicious." I nodded to the locker room, where several of the monks were undressing.

"Close it, damnit!" The biceps of his fully extended arms swelled under the weight. Sweat plastered the hair on his naked chest and abdomen. "Take this."

V

I placed the barbell on its rest and sat on a plastic chair, scuffed from use. Michael sat up and wiped his face with a white towel. I could smell the bleach in it, used heavily by the pathetic monk who did the laundry.

"The federal agent talked to me today." Michael spoke in a hushed voice despite the private room.

"Andrews?"

"Yes. He had all kinds of questions about you, and about the two of us."

"Why should he care about two homosexual monks? Isn't finding a serial killer enough for him?" Nonchalant, I hoisted my feet up on the other bench.

"It's got something to do with finding Luke. He apparently knows about your relationship with him."

"Yes, he asked me about it."

"He wanted to know if there was anything unusual about you."

"Unusual? In what way?"

Michael shrugged. "Seems like he wanted to know if you indulge in some form of sadism. He seems to suspect you."

"Of scaring Luke away from the monastery? I know that. Good agent Andrews made that clear in our chat."

"It's more than that." Michael scooted down the bench, closer to me. He leaned over on his knees. "This is incredible, but I think he suspects you of killing Luke."

"What!"

"He made me show him my arms and back to prove you'd never abused me. He asked about your weird ideas, about your occult beliefs. Victor, I think he bugged your cell. That's why I wanted to talk here."

My face and manner remained calm, while fury welled in me like electricity in a stormy sky ready to burst forth in lightning. The news confirmed my fears about the car I'd seen slip

V

behind the trees. Michael and I were under surveillance.

"Victor, I want the truth." Michael's eyes were unflinching in their intensity. "Did you hurt Luke more than emotionally?"

"Why don't you ask your real question?" I shouted. "Did I kill Luke and cut him up in pieces? You think I'm the killer stalking the woods?"

Michael remained unintimidated by my rage. "I don't think anything. I only want to hear from your own lips that you didn't harm Luke."

I glared at him. "I thought you loved me. Do you?"

"Yes, God help me. But I understand you, the extremes of your passions. You're capable of anything. That's what drew me to you. And your strength."

I broke into a laugh. "I see what this is all about. I've always known it. You got Luke out of your way, just to have me for yourself. Now you have qualms of conscience. That's very unbecoming of you, Michael. I thought you were above petty scrupulosity."

My words hit my mark, as I knew they would. He calmly studied me. "I'm not above shame."

"Relax, Michael." I slapped his arm. "I'm not a psychopath. Unless my own life were at stake, I wouldn't waste my time killing anyone."

Brooding, Michael stood, pulled on his T-shirt, and opened the door.

I laughed again.

"What?" he said, irritated.

"You look like Judas Iscariot."

He dismissed me with a glance and walked out.

"It's not worth hanging yourself over," I shouted after him and broke into a fit of laughter.

Back in my cell, I turned over the bed and pulled the books from their shelves in search of the listening device. I stood on a

V

chair to inspect the painted pipe that ran the length of the ceiling and rummaged through the desk drawers. I was just about to fling the crucifix down after searching the back of it when I noticed the tiny case behind the bent knees of the corpus.

The irony of my enemy's means of spying did not escape me. Not only had Joshu fled from me, but his image assisted my would-be captors.

In that moment I craved the blood of the arrogant agent, who even now listened to my excited breathing. My fangs shot forth in anticipation as I stormed up the crypt stairs and down the winding drive. The white sedan was exactly where I expected it to be. In wrinkled starched shirts, Andrews and another agent got out of the car when they saw me approaching, both with their hands near the guns on their hips.

"Evening, Brother Victor. Can we help you with something?" Andrews had been eating a sandwich. He dabbed his lips with a handkerchief.

Andrew's partner was 40ish and balding, but a large, well-built man. I could have lunged at them in an instant, their blood titillated me so.

"You've invaded my privacy, Mr. Andrews." I held out the recorder, then hurled it off into the trees. "If you want excitement, go get yourselves fucked."

"Something right up your alley, isn't it, Brother?" Andrews sneered at me.

His neck, rising firm and thick from his loosened collar, beckoned to me in that moment. My fangs, which had retracted, inched forward again, and only through enormous concentration could I control their growth. As I turned to avoid any more temptation, Andrews called me back.

"Where are you from, Brother Victor?" He emphasized the word "Brother" in a mocking tone.

V

I stopped and faced him.

"You think you'll hide your tracks long?" He leaned against the car now. The other agent had relaxed too.

"The abbot has my records. I'm sure you've already seen them."

"Records from a monastery that no longer exists? A letter from a dead abbot?"

I smiled at the cockiness behind his transparent ploy to goad me into desperation now that the FBI was on my trail. I swore to myself that I would have that man eventually, then retraced my steps to the monastery.

The next day the evening news covered my most recent slayings, neighbors only that day having discovered the bodies of the crippled man and his mother. Cameras scanned the scene, the empty bed and wheelchair, the bodies being carried out in black bags. The elderly couple who had found the corpses explained that when the son hadn't emerged for his usual spins around the block, they'd knocked on the door. That failing, they'd tried without luck to reach him by phone. Then, finding the broken door in back, they ventured in.

At this point the old woman, wearing a sweatshirt stamped with the words "Proud to be a Grandma," broke into tears. "Oh, sweet Jesus! I never seen such a thing in my life."

Her husband, pushing up a pair of thick glasses, wrapped his arm around her.

The lanky blond reporter asked him how long they had known the victims.

The old man shook his head. "Mr. and Mrs. Sanders lived here when we bought the house back in '48. Jimmy came along a couple years later. Always playing soldier out in the yard here. A good boy. Took care of his mama after his daddy died." The man was too choked up to go on.

The maudlin curiosity of the monks annoyed me, and I had

V

no desire to watch the rest of the coverage. But to leave now, with the abbot entertaining fears about me because of the FBI's probings, would have drawn unnecessary attention to myself.

A shot of the man's Marine photograph flashed on the screen, followed by an interview of a Paris Island officer, who attested to the soldier's dedication in boot camp and then in Vietnam, where an exploding land mine left him a paraplegic.

When the reporter interviewed Andrews, I swore he was looking directly at me.

"Yes, we are following some leads," he said in response to the reporter's question. He wore a navy-blue suit and a tie with neat rows of print—straight and controlled. "But we are not at liberty to discuss our suspects. We want to assure the community that we are doing everything within our power to get this fiend."

"Is it true, Lieutenant Andrews, that the blood was drained from these victims? That the killer is a member of a vampire cult?"

"We are not at liberty to discuss details of the investigation." Andrews's boyish face remained expressionless, his tone official.

"Could you tell us anything about the monk from St. Thomas Monastery, Brother Luke McMahan? A missing person's report has been filed with the police. Do you suspect foul play in this case?" The eager reporter tucked her straight hair behind her ear.

Andrews started looking impatient now. "The local police are handling that case. There is no evidence of foul play at this point."

The subject stirred the monks to comment and sigh and chat over their cocktails. Two younger monks appeared to take out their frustration over Luke on a ping-pong ball, which they knocked mercilessly back and forth across the net. Michael glanced at me from the open window, where he'd been musing over an illuminated fountain of John the Baptist in the Jordan.

I wanted air. Before evening prayer I strolled out to the

V

courtyard. Daffodils had already bloomed and hedges of for-
sythia clustered around the oak, which had started to bud. I sat
on a stone bench, closed my eyes, and inhaled the cool air stir-
ring the skirts of my habit. No moon glowed, but even so I felt
its magnetic power upon my immortal blood and reveled in the
vision of the realm ever bathed in its illumination.

This was the last time I'd be forced into a corner, waging
battle against human enemies that snapped at me like dogs. I
was weary of it. From Jerusalem to Athens to Nampo; from
Mozambique to Brindisi in the heel of Italy to the villages of
Alsace-Lorraine and the hamlets of England; I'd traveled across
the globe for 2,000 years, powerful but hunted, and I was now
ready for my eternal reward. This time I would not flee the
region, but the mortal sphere itself.

Twenty-five

Holy Week nauseated me. The scripture readings about Joshu's triumphant entry into Jerusalem (if you call 20 beggars and a handful of religious fanatics fluttering palm branches triumphant); his romanticized last supper with 12 laborers who reeked of fish; him sweating blood in Gethsemane (more palatable than saying he was ready to soil himself from fear). The early Christian movement had spun the whole train of mundane events into a myth surpassing the epic of Aeneas.

But Good Friday revolted me the most. The rituals and readings reveling in the gore dripping from Joshu's face, hands, and feet because with it flowed his life, the prerequisite of redemption; this maudlin sentimentality perverted real passion

V

for the sinewy man, wasting the blood that should have been lapped up as the fuel of orgasm.

Who on this damnable earth, millennia after his death, could lust for the man Joshu?

When I crept from my tomb the night of Good Friday, the chapel above seemed to press like a weight on my back. On their knees, amidst clouds of incense, the monks had observed the sacred hours from noon to 3—when Joshu expired—loading the vaulted space with, for me, a tangible perversion of my love.

Now, tested and watched, I had to ascend and join their desecrating rituals.

Purple cloth swathed every statue in the dimly lit chapel. The tabernacle door stood wide open, the ciborium of communion wafers removed to commemorate Joshu's arrest and removal from Gethsemane. The marble altar had been stripped of its linen.

When evening service began the monks rose, black figures in the shadows. Swinging a censer by its chain, Michael led the procession down the center aisle. His bleached surplice set off his dark brows and hair, his olive complexion. His face showed his absorption in the ritual.

The abbot brought up the rear of the procession, lifting a crucifix that was three feet tall and shrouded in purple.

"Behold the wood of the cross," he chanted, "on which is hung our salvation."

"Come, let us adore," responded the monks, dropping to their knees.

The invocation and refrain were repeated twice more, each time the abbot exposing another arm or leg of the plaster corpus until, upon reaching the sanctuary, he hoisted up a crucifix completely bared.

When the monks filed from the stalls to kiss the feet of the

V

corpus, I fought the impulse to rush forward and crush the plaster figure. When my turn came to genuflect before the cross, while the abbot held it on the sanctuary step, I shot a glance at Michael. He stood by with a linen napkin to wipe the feet after each kiss.

"Yes, Victor," his eyes said to me. Was he directing me to offer the ritual kiss, or was he expressing assent? If so, to what?

I took a breath and brushed my lips against the cold feet. By the time I returned to my stall, I knew the moment had come. Michael must tour the Dark Kingdom.

When he came to my cell just before midnight, I was sitting in the soft illumination of candles burning in all four corners of the room. Michael closed the door softly behind him and glanced around. The bed was stripped, my books packed back in the trunk. The crucifix rose from the wastebasket.

"What's going on, Victor?" Michael wore a black sweatshirt and black jeans, a modernized habit of sorts.

"I want to take you to the place now." I'd tipped back the chair to rest my feet on the bed.

"The Dark Kingdom?" Michael leaned against the desk. "Why now?"

"It's the right moment. Will you go?"

He paused and studied the wall. "Strange. I feel exactly the way I did the day I entered the monastery. A step into the unknown."

"Very appropriate." I lowered my feet and leaned forward to take his hands in mine. "Believe me, once you see it, your life will change. Immortality will mean something. Not pious garbage about eternal peace. You weren't made for peace and neither was I. Our souls are strong, violent, passionate."

"And evil?"

"Evil. What does that mean?" The word disgusted me. "Rebellion against the Christian god, who rules with an iron hand, twists souls into his own image and likeness, demands

V

from them unyielding devotion to no one but him? Is that evil? What about black skies scorned by sailors as they approach the rocks, winds that strip a field of grain? Are they evil, or are they simply power? Why moralize about strength and passion?"

"Take me," Michael said in a whisper, his dark eyes willful, excited.

I stood and stripped off my T-shirt and sweatpants. "Come here."

I pulled off his shirt, caressed his exquisite pectorals and biceps. Our heated lips met, our tongues pressing past each other's lips like impatient serpents entering their lairs. Then I pulled him to the bed and directed his mouth to my nipple, as Tiresia had directed me to hers centuries before monks came into being. He sucked, tenderly at first, and then as blood squirted down his throat, greedily, wantonly.

My head spun. I abandoned myself to the movement, which took an upward turn, like the takeoff of a plane, gracefully piercing an ebony sky. Michael's position had changed now. From behind me he hugged my waist, his face against my neck, as I rocketed moonward. He moaned in delight, gasped for air.

When we entered a sea of silver light, our momentum slowed. We floated now, over a wall, over tiled roofs gleaming under the dreamy light.

"It's Rome," I cried. "Rome restored."

Below us the Tiber snaked through the spires and domes, past the round Castel San Angelo, its crenellated tower near the riverbank, where pines swayed in the warm current above the river. Along the water, lovers embraced, their nude bodies perfectly proportional, strong, supple.

The marble facing of the Coliseum, torn away by the invading Visigoths, again covered it like shiny pink armor, and the noble buildings and columns and squares of the Forum were

V

risen from the melancholy rubble. Medieval churches were restored too, their facades shimmering in the moonlight along the narrow streets. Crowds of spectators roared over gladiators in the Circus Maximus, whose sculpted muscles were as beautiful as their movements when they dodged and thrust the sword. And from the Pantheon, the sphere of perfection, haunting mantras to the gods rippled across the Piazza Navona, whose elliptical perimeter enclosed sword-eaters, lute-players, men at game tables, boys splashing through the waters of Bernini's fountain, women laughing with abandon as they inspected jewels on display in canvas-covered booths.

The colossal structures, the marble columns and Egyptian obelisks claimed as battle trophies, the noble shapes and movements of bare human forms, as breathtaking as statues and yet as flexible and rapid as the Tiber as it empties into the Ostian harbor, the eerie light cast on the city and its vital inhabitants by a white moon, round and precious as a giant jewel lying on velvet—all these things lent an awesome sublimity to the world we surveyed as we glided through space.

"Did you know this?" Michael yelled into the wind, panting, sweating against my body. "Did you know it would be like this?"

I shook my head. "It's beyond my wildest dreams."

Laughter caught my ear and when I turned, Tiresia moved through the air next to me, her dark skin spangled with jewels, a crown of rubies and emeralds glittering on her head. "Yes, Victor, it's time. What more could you want?" She stretched her hands, arched her smooth back, and dove down to a courtyard, where she mounted a boy stretched out on the ground and soon convulsed in pleasure as she rode him.

"I've waited centuries for this!" I shouted. "Now, with you, I can take my rightful reward. Laughter, sensuality, beauty, action. Action, Michael, action. For eternity."

V

He tightened his grip around me as his body trembled spasmodically against mine.

A moment later, we lay entwined once again in my cell, our chests heaving as though we'd run a race and collapsed beyond the finish line.

VII
Revelation

Twenty-six

"Two millennia?" Michael strained to comprehend the length of my history.

"Since the reign of Caesar Augustus, yes."

It was the night following our journey, the first chance to discuss an experience that had exhausted us both. We walked through the woods, where buds swelled on the oaks and maples stretching their arms after winter's dormancy into the sweet air of spring.

For the first time in my nocturnal existence, I unfolded the entire story of my origins, earthly and supernatural—Rome, Jerusalem, Tiresia, the roaming of the world's monasteries and the obsession that took me within their walls until that very moment. My means of nourishment I left for later.

V

"Joshu," he said. "Because it's closer to the Hebrew." He had listened silently as we hiked, until now.

"I wanted him as much as a soul can want."

"In love with Jesus of Nazareth." Michael mused over the idea. "The Christ."

"That's what history has called him. I knew the boy, the man of flesh and blood. The man who laughed at my crude jokes. The man who raced me across the Jordan. The man with pimples on his back. It's taken me 2,000 years to replace him."

"Incarnation. Incarnation." Michael murmured the word.

"What? What are you talking about?" I grabbed his arm to stop him.

"Nothing. I don't know. This is too much to take in."

Impatient with his musings, I leveled my eyes with his. "The point, Michael, is that you must inherit my existence. Wander here a brief time, then join me in that kingdom we've inspected. That's all that matters. Our eternity together."

"What do you mean inherit your existence?" He seemed to snap out of his contemplation, his eyes now sharp as a lawyer's.

"I mean this." I raised my hands. "The night. To live in the night until it's time to join me."

"Never see the sun again?"

"No. To hell with the sun!" I let go of him and took a few steps away to cool myself before turning back to him. "You want mortality when you can live forever? You'll have the power to take what you want. Anything. Then you'll go on living, really living, for eternity."

"But I wouldn't be mortal here. I'd become…whatever kind of being you are. Those are the terms?"

"Yes. You would have my powers. You could communicate with me."

"You're not telling me everything."

V

"What!"

"Everything, Victor." He drew close to me and clasped my arms, his eyes inches from mine. "There's still a closed door. Once again, you expect me to surrender, but you put up a wall. I'll take nothing less than everything, or there's nothing more to discuss."

I pushed him away. "Damn you. You want to know what it's taken me centuries to learn, is that it? A shortcut? I'm telling you, you can't understand it all now. Not until you are what I am. I can only promise you a freedom and power you've never known. Isn't that enough?"

"It's you I want, only you."

I laughed deeply and kissed him hard on the lips.

Over the next week, I made arrangements for Michael's new existence. His affection for New Orleans directed my search for lodgings there, not far from the above-ground tombs of St. Louis Cemetery, where his beloved Jana was buried and where he could easily claim the coffin of a new corpse and a forgotten mausoleum as his sleeping chamber. From a Swiss account, I transferred funds to a local bank in the French Quarter. Over the centuries I'd added to Tiresia's treasure through robbery and investment.

As for monastery life, that was up to Michael. He wouldn't share my initial motive for seeking cloisters, though he was drawn to the secluded life and would find in them companionship of sorts, as I had.

How would he take the life of predator, ripping into throats of children, women, crippled war veterans? He would adjust. Survival was survival, wherever you stood in the food chain. I counted on his supernatural cravings, his philosophical perspective, his passionate nature—these could obliterate mortal sensibility, which focused on the petty, the particular. I counted on his union with my soul to stir a sublime storm whose winds would devastate the oppressive claims of conscience. But for

V

now, he must know nothing of my bloody nourishment. Before its strangulation, his conscience could misguide him, shrinking into a narrow chink his mind's all-encompassing window.

Michael Schiefelbein

Twenty-seven

Easter lilies around the altar, the moist, clean smell of the season of love—it was the first time in a monastery that I'd caught the excitement of resurrection. Not Joshu's, which I'd cursed over the centuries, but stirrings, nonetheless, that only he had raised in me before now. A longing deep in my immortal core, echoed by warm wind when it rushed over the mountains and through the pines and maples, by spring rain falling like Chopin's melodies. A longing that promised completion, though it could never be truly completed.

We prolonged the time before my departure, the days before his death and new existence. If centuries should pass before he joined me, we wanted to spend them anticipating a continua-

V

tion of an interrupted love affair. In balmy air or thunderstorms, under moonlit or raven skies, we haunted the woods together, laughed as we pitched stones at bats spilling from hillside caves, made heated love in abandoned shacks.

One night in early May, Michael challenged me to a race on the footpath where he'd disappeared before. The moon, directly overhead, washed the ground with pale light.

"Don't make me laugh," I said. "What are your chances against me?"

He surveyed me arrogantly. "Let's just see." He pulled off his shirt and deposited a stick on the path. "That's the starting line. Are you ready?"

We positioned ourselves, and at the count of three, shot forward.

At first I held back, giving him a chance to gain ground so I could pass him more impressively. His arms pumped furiously, his feet kicked up high behind him, his dark ponytail bounced.

When he'd covered a good half-mile, I launched forward, speeding past the trees, reaching the apex of the hill in a matter of seconds. But when I got to where Michael should have been, I spotted him in the distance, at a curve in the path. Then he vanished behind the foliage.

Accelerating to my full speed, I gained the bend in seconds and intended to tug his ponytail, but once again he was relentlessly sprinting far ahead of me.

When I reached a rocky ledge, he was sitting on the ground, waiting for me. Winded, I dropped down beside him.

"Is this a trick Jana taught you?" I asked when I'd finally caught my breath.

"How did you guess?" He grinned and leaned back on his elbows. "I've got a surprise for you, another trick. Watch the sky."

The sweep of the wooded gray valley rolling to the horizon was magnificent. The river glinted through the branches. The

V

monastery buildings huddled in a clearing and to the south, a black train threaded in and out of the trees, its lonely whistle piercing the silence.

Suddenly the pale sky brightened, as though the sun rose from the west, just beyond the horizon. "What!" I shot to my feet, ready to fly back to my dark refuge.

"Wait!" Michael grabbed my hand. "It's not real. Come on, sit down and enjoy something you haven't seen in a few centuries."

Light suffused the sky now, a sky bluer and clearer than I had remembered. Birds twittered in the false morning light.

"Now look there." Michael pointed to the eastern sky, where a ball of light blazed, my enemy in all his glory. Heat bathed my face, my arms and hands, as though I were on a beach near Positano rather than a mountainside at midnight.

The flaming sun shrank and the blue sky changed to indigo and then to silver as the moon resumed her post.

"Impressive," I said.

"It's my pledge to you, Victor. I have to admit, no one has ever affected me like you do. I've always been a detached spirit, drawing what I could from every circle I found myself in. I don't want to call it coldness or fear. It's just that I felt satisfied— working with the soil, studying philosophical discourses, drinking in the waters of mysticism. But now," he hesitated, lowering his eyes, "now I breath you like air. You're Patroclus to me."

"So you're Achilles? I like that." I grinned, and then clasped both his hands. "I've waited for this moment, night after night, century after century."

On the rocky ledge, the moon falling to the west, we entwined ourselves more like wrestlers than lovers, heaving, pressing, squeezing, and grunting, more primitive than the animals populating the woods around us. More than once, Michael's lips found my nipple, and each time the ecstasy his

V

mouth brought to me almost numbed me to the danger of letting him drink too much of my blood.

"No," I finally said, each time, pushing his head away. "I'm not ready to leave you yet."

We stayed in the spot until the light of dawn bled into the sky above the mountains. I'd lost track of the time and now every cell in my body was alert to the imminent danger. His head on my chest, Michael had fallen asleep. I shook him.

"We've got to hurry. It's almost dawn." Scooping him up in my arms, I willed us to the monastery grounds. Branches gave way to us, the air formed a vacuum with the velocity of our movement.

As we raced to the entrance, Andrews's white sedan pulled up. He got out and motioned for us to wait for him.

"Go ahead," Michael said. "I'll talk to him."

With no other choice, I hurried to the crypt, my skin stinging from exposure to the predawn radiation.

Twenty-eight

Because Andrews watched my every move—as he emphasized to Michael the night of the sun show—my feedings required caution, mostly to prevent him from knowing when I left the grounds. I had to initiate my flight from within the courtyard, where I also returned at the end of my hunts. I could give him no grounds for linking me to the crime scenes investigated day after day in a city frozen by fear.

One night in late April, I stole through a poorly lit neighborhood of housing projects in the city. Ducking into shadows whenever a patrol car whirled its searchlight, I sniffed for a large concentration of blood to keep me satisfied for a number of days, reducing the number of risky trips. Just when I caught the scent of

V

a mass of blood in one of the dilapidated apartments, a searchlight shot out from a police car hidden behind a tree in an empty lot. I moaned in pain at the intensity of light, too stunned to move.

"Police! Put your hands up!" an officer shouted from the car.

I couldn't see him for the light, but I heard footsteps and voices on the street. The smell of blood laced with alcohol wafted from his direction. I waited with my hands raised as he'd commanded.

By the time he started frisking me, while his partner pointed his gun at me, my pain had subsided and I was able to concentrate. I had no choice now that they'd seen me. In two moves I'd flung them both to the ground. I'd snapped the neck of the first officer when the second recovered his gun and fired, hitting me in the shoulder. Before he could shoot again I grabbed the gun from him and snapped his neck. Between the two of them, both hefty men, I could drain more than enough blood. But the shot had roused the neighborhood. A siren wailed only streets away.

I reached the opposite end of town in seconds, lighting near a park. A colonial home across the street emitted the sanguinary scent of at least two people. With no time for a more leisurely hunt, I broke into a side door hidden by a trellis and found myself in a richly furnished parlor dominated by a grand piano. Before proceeding to the bedrooms, I sank into a white sofa to rest while I healed. The bullet wound of a vampire closes in minutes, the missile itself disintegrating as soon as it penetrates the skin.

The floor was littered with wrapping paper. Empty drink glasses cluttered the tables. I picked up a greeting card from a stack on the coffee table, wishing Diane and Paul a happy 25th wedding anniversary. I could exhibit mercy, but under the circumstances I needed to feed and flee the city. Once I'd recovered, I crept down a carpeted hallway and up a staircase. The scent of blood swelled as I approached the last door, which was shut. With my ear against the door, I listened to gentle groaning

V

and squeaking springs within. At the moment of climax, I opened the door.

The man's white body covered his wife's. Her legs were wrapped around his. He couldn't make me out in the pitch-black room, though of course I could discern his panicked expression as he glanced toward the door.

"Jimmy? Wait a minute, son." He rolled off his wife and grabbed his robe. She pulled the sheets up.

Now the pungent scent of semen and female secretions joined the smell of blood. My fangs shot forth and I lunged greedily at his throat.

"No!" The woman screamed. Scampering naked from the bed, she bolted out the door. I cut her off at the bottom of the staircase, where I had willed myself.

"Please!" she sobbed, dropping to her knees. "Oh, God, please!"

Although she was probably in her late 40s, she was quite alluring. I stroked her long, soft hair and raised her chin to me, as her body continued to convulse. Her breasts were large and round, the nipples unusually large. I pulled her up by the arms and dragged her to the open hallway, where I fell upon her breasts as she cried for me to stop. Licking the nipples gently for a moment, I finally pierced through the tender flesh and lapped up the blood. Then I turned to her throat, but before I could drink, footsteps pounded down the stairs.

"Mom, where are you?" a boy called in the darkness. When he reached the hallway, he flicked on the light. He was 15 or 16, in a sweatshirt and shorts. "My God!" He disappeared into the sitting room and came out brandishing a fireplace poker.

"Get off her!" He drew back the poker as though he would run it through me. "Mom, are you all right?" His body trembled.

The unconscious woman remained motionless. I stood and stepped toward the boy. "She's just asleep."

V

When he jabbed at me with the poker, I wrenched it from his hands. I gripped his shoulders and drew his face up to mine and inhaled his luscious scent. His eyes were wide with horror.

"You're quite a specimen," I said. I kissed his full lips and sank my fangs into his neck. He instantly went limp.

When I had drunk every drop in his body, I returned to his mother to drain her. Between the two of them I was more than satiated. Even if the man upstairs had not already chilled to a dangerous point for drinking blood I wouldn't have touched him.

I left them all where they had died and exited through the same door I'd entered. Sirens howled throughout the city. Searchlights flashed up the street and scanned the park. Just as a patrol car turned the corner, I rose into the air and sped across the miles between Knoxville and the monastery.

It was nearly 3 o'clock when I returned. I crossed through the dark chapel on my way to the crypt. Exhausted from the killings, bloated with blood, I wanted to sleep though dawn was still a few hours away. But when I crawled into my coffin in the close, dark mausoleum, I lay awake for a long time, disturbed by something—not the killings, but a presence, like the presence I had felt once before outside my tomb, a presence that had amused me then. Now it threatened my dreams.

Michael Schiefelbein

Twenty-nine

At dusk, as though electricity surged through me, my furious heart awakened me. He waited for me outside the tomb. The iron door squealed like a rat as I pushed it open to face Michael, who watched as intensely as the Roman sentinels outside the tomb of Joshu.

"Exactly dusk," he said as I emerged. He sat on the cold floor, against a stone pillar. The meager incandescent lights lacked the strength to wipe the shadow from his face.

"So, you know?" I stretched and rubbed my eyes.

"I watched you come in, just after Andrews sped into town. I couldn't sleep. I was out walking. He and the other agent had apparently been searching for you here. But they didn't look long before they gave up and took off down the drive. I waited until you got back. I knew you'd be coming."

"Michael, I've put off explaining—"

He raised his hand to interrupt me. "Everything was confirmed this evening on the news. Three corpses, two drained of blood. A patrol car cruising the area spotted a suspicious man, then checked the houses on the street."

I squinted to see his eyes. "Come to my cell. Let me explain it from the beginning."

"We can't miss dinner and vespers, Victor. The last thing you need is to stir up any more suspicion here. We can talk later."

I grabbed his arm as he started to get up. "You don't blame me, then."

"Nature is nature."

"I adore you, Michael." I shook his arm.

The evening dragged. We chanted the longest, dreariest psalms at vespers. At dinner, the reading from *Lives of the Saints* detailed the martyrdom of St. Lawrence, who praised God while he was grilled to death. Talk of the killings dominated the social hour. Neighbors of the victims were interviewed on the news and Andrews once again assured the city that the murderer would be apprehended. When the reporter pressed him about the killer's identity, Andrews refused to share the details he claimed to have.

As much as Andrews suspected me in Luke's disappearance, surely by now he'd given up trying to pin the mountain and Knoxville murders on me. After all, he'd never seen me leave the monastery grounds. Or maybe he thought I had a partner in the city. But none of that mattered. I focused on setting things right with Michael and preparing for his baptism into the night.

Grave, intense, Michael fired question after question at me

V

when we met in the library's stacks after the Grand Silence had begun. We sat on the age-darkened plank floor between shelves of books, the humid air full of their smell. Thunder rumbled above us.

"This author traces vampires to Satan." Michael picked up one of the volumes piled next to him. "Is it true?"

"Satan, the fallen angel? No, he took a different route than the founder of the Dark Kingdom. He wanted to usurp the role of heaven's god. He wanted an eternity of adoration—static, lifeless worship. The Dark Kingdom is a place of activity, as you've seen."

"Heaven's god? There's more than one?"

"Many powers rule the universe. Nations take their pick—Isis, Zeus, the Hebrew god. I'm no enemy of the gods. They are simply not relevant to me. They exist in spheres not accessible to me, just as mine is not accessible to them."

"Your food, Victor. All these people. The killings in the mountains too, I suppose. What is it like?" He spoke with the burning interest underlying all his quests for knowledge.

I shrugged. "Sometimes exhilarating, sometimes…sometimes unpleasant."

"You killed Luke, didn't you?"

"It was unavoidable. He threatened to expose me, to have me expelled. It was a matter of survival."

He looked away for a moment before speaking again, in nearly a whisper. "And you drank his blood?"

"Yes. It's how I live. How you will live, Michael. As you say, nature is nature. If you give in to petty scruples, see through mortal eyes, it's abhorrent. But look at the wolves. Look at human's killing for meat. Vampires live on blood."

"Vampires." Michael pondered the word. "Jana spoke of creatures of the night. Are there others? Do you have enemies, allies?"

He'd asked the question I dreaded most. To condemn him to

V

a life of solitude, the most torturous aspect of my existence, how could he understand?

"Yes, there are others. But we operate alone, until we create a successor." I paused, then said, "What are decades or centuries, though, when compared to eternity?" I leaned forward and clasped his shoulders. "Besides, in the interim you can live on our passion, Michael. I lived without it all this time on earth. Now I think I could stay another 2,000 years, if I knew I would be joining you."

"Will I be able to communicate with you?"

"I can make no promises. I don't know enough."

"What if we both stay here? What if we leave this place and make a life somewhere else?"

"You mean until you die?"

"Yes. Can't I share your existence now? These books talk about large numbers of vampires."

"Forget the books!" I pounded a shelf with my fist. "I'm telling you it's not a choice. Other vampires exist, but all rule their own domains. We never come into contact. We can't. There's a barrier."

Michael gazed at me steadily, despite the excitement and fear I detected pulsing through him. "How can I live without you for centuries?"

"You are strong enough to do it. And there's no choice."

"And feeding on people—"

"You'll do it. We all do it. The blood: There's nothing like it, the sense of elation, the power. To think the life of a man is pouring into you. Think of communion, for God's sake. The hunger for blood takes people there. The blood of a victim. Remember the taste of my blood, Michael?"

"But you weren't a victim."

V

I laughed. "You're wrong. You held complete power over my soul."

As the thunder rolled and exploded, rain pelted the roof. Our niche among the books was a snug refuge that, in light of our impending separation, took on the romance of a dark bedroom the day before a battle.

Aware of our alliance in subversion, united in blood and the dark longings of our souls, we fell into each other's arms. I stripped off his shorts and T-shirt and buried my face in his musky crotch, licking the dark sack, the thick cock. My tongue traced the line of dark fur from that sweet meat to his chest, where it densely swirled. Our lips met, then our tongues. We wrestled playfully. He finally sat upon my belly, pinning back my arms, and impaled himself upon my rigid cock. Massaging his own, he groaned in his motion, and I, panting in the scent of his racing blood, groaned too, until we both exploded in orgasm.

Thirty

In the midst of the relentless media coverage of the devastation wrought by the "vampire killer," as I was dubbed by the press, Luke's grandfather visited the monastery. The dotard had to see where his boy last lived, had to search the woods himself. Apparently, Brother Matthew had discouraged his coming, but to no avail.

During compline, he sat in Luke's choir stall, glum and distracted, not bothering to follow the psalms in his grandson's breviary, which he caressed as though it were a child. He was a tall, rawboned man in his mid-60s, with deep grooves in his tanned cheeks and close-cropped gray hair. He wore a short-sleeved plaid shirt and blue jeans—a farmer through and

V

through. From dawn to dusk he'd trekked through the woods, Michael told me, without stopping to eat, and had only picked at his food during dinner.

When the moment came for petitions, he spoke up wearily, in what I by now recognized as a country accent.

"I wanna ask the Lord to lead me to my boy. If he's dead, I just wanna know. But I pray he's alive. He ain't never hurt nobody. Looks like a killer wouldn't have no use for him, but I don't guess that matters to a pervert. I know it ain't right to wish evil on nobody, but I ask the Lord to strike that monster down in his tracks, afore he can kill another soul."

After compline, Michael spoke to him, briefly clasping his shoulder. It was a mistake to allow this compassion. Why stir the waters? A general could not weep over the slain soldiers on the field, whether his own men or those of the enemy. He must harden himself against future losses, future massacres. But I knew for now it was asking too much. With time Michael would see the necessity of leaving uncompromised the detachment natural to him.

What concerned me more was the incredible susceptibility of Michael's soul to supernatural interference. When he failed to show up at my cell that night at the appointed hour, I ventured to his. Flames encased in red glass flickered throughout his room and sweet incense smoked densely. Michael lay naked on the floor, his arms outstretched. The shadow of the crucifix suspended in midair above him fell across his face. His cock was swollen with blood. As before, he invoked the cross, instrument of torture, as a source of hope.

"O crux, ave spes unica." His tone was insistent, as if he were leading a war cry, and he repeated the pronouncement again and again as though accompanied by a battle drum.

I wanted to interrupt the spell, shake him from his vision,

V

but once again I could not penetrate the invisible wall between us. Frustrated, I stood near the door.

The chant quickened, gaining urgency, and then stopped abruptly, as though the enemies now stood eye to eye, ready to charge across the battlefield. He got up on his knees, extending his arms before the crucifix, apparently receiving from it a burden. Straining under the invisible weight he stood and approached the door, which swung open of its own accord when I stepped aside. I followed him down the dark corridor, alert to any movements behind the closed doors, particularly the door of the abbot's cell.

I followed him all the way down the stairs to the crypt and through the long, dank passage to my tomb, where he stopped.

He grimaced as if in great pain, sweat beading on his forehead. He moaned like a frustrated dumb man trying to communicate. It was the iron gate, I knew; he wanted it opened and I obliged him. That calmed him. Standing naked before the black mouth of the mausoleum, his arms still extended, he appeared to wait for someone to relieve him of his heavy treasure. I followed his cue, pantomiming a transfer of the burden from his arms to mine.

When he motioned to the tomb, I pretended to lay what must have been a corpse inside. Tears streamed down his face. Then he opened his eyes and the weeping ceased.

"He's here, Victor." He whispered, his eyes on the gaping tomb.
"Yes."

"He called out to me. Then I found him in the woods, white as chalk."

"This is a temptation, Michael." I laid my hand on his shoulder. "Joshu wants you for himself. But for what? So you can kneel with him before his father's throne for all eternity?"

He turned his head slowly until our eyes met. "Yes. There was

V

something in the vision about Jesus. At first there were colors—red, yellow, black splashed against a white screen, and then a cross, a writing body, and then Luke lay before me in the woods."

Securing the iron gate, I led Michael to my cell, where I directed him to wait until I could retrieve his clothes. When I returned with his shorts and T-shirt, he was rolling his head as if to relieve tension from his neck and shoulders.

"Let's take a walk," I said.

He nodded, alert now after the long trance.

The grass, taller after a week of rain, formed a soft carpet beneath our feet. Light-green leaves budded on the trees scattered across the grounds. The sour smell of mulch wafted on a warm breeze cascading over the mountains.

Once secure inside the woods, I took Michael's hand as we climbed through the leafing oaks, over stumps and fallen trunks. Only a slice of moon jeweled the sky, so it was up to me to guide him through the black thicket to our clearing.

"Your gloom's because of our parting," I said when we had settled on the ground against the log. "And once you're transformed the visions will stop."

"How do you know? How do you know these things?"

"Don't question me," I said firmly. "Give yourself over. A divided soul can't survive."

"Yes, I know." He laid his head back against the log and studied the sky. "This has to happen soon, Victor. I won't permit my soul to be used as a battleground for invisible forces. But there is one thing." He turned to me. "I want to sleep with you."

"Sleep?"

"Next to your coffin. I want to spend our final hours together. At dusk when we wake up this thing has to happen."

I studied his keen eyes, in search of ulterior motives, but without success. "Is this a test run? Do you want to make sure

V

you can survive sleeping among the dead?"

"I've told you what I want."

"All right. At dawn we sleep."

When the sky lightened behind the mountains, we climbed down to the crypt. I entered the tomb first and made space for him near my coffin. He lay calmly, quietly, while I shut the gate. I loosened a brick in the back wall to let in air from a narrow channel between the mausoleums and the outer wall of the foundation. Then I climbed into my bed.

"How are you?" I asked.

"Fine. The dead don't frighten me."

"You know, in some medieval monasteries monks had to build their own coffins and sleep in them every night."

"Yes, I know, to remind them of their mortality."

"For you it's a promise of eternity."

I squeezed his hand and fell into the most peaceful sleep I'd had in two centuries.

Just before dusk, though, I dreamed of Luke. He stood over us in the tomb, naked, pale. He sobbed. Putrid blood dripped from his throat onto Michael's face. Michael's eyes snapped open. In a feverous delirium he struggled to escape from the tomb. I awoke and realized that it was no dream. Kneeling over my coffin, he pummeled my chest.

I seized his wrists. "Wake up. It's a dream."

"I am awake. I am." He stopped struggling against me and took a deep breath.

"Don't let Luke haunt you."

"It's not Luke. It's something else. I dreamed of heaven."

"What? Some fantasy?"

"No. I don't know." He settled back on his haunches. "I can't do it, Victor."

"What! What do you mean?"

        Michael Schiefelbein

V

"I can't."

"You're babbling like an idiot. Get out in the air and calm yourself."

"It won't help. My sense is strong. This can't be done."

"What, is your Jana putting crazy ideas in your head? Fuck her. You love me. That's what matters. A magnificent life is ahead of us. You won't back out, not if you listen to your own desires instead of a spirit's black magic."

But his gaze was one of resolution, not fear.

"It's useless to discuss it now," I said. "Get out. We'll talk tomorrow."

He said nothing as he crawled from the tomb.

VIII
The Storm

Thirty-one

That night was the darkest, longest I'd known in my centuries of flight from the sun. Restless to the point of madness, I heard the subtlest movements in the woods, smelled the decay of animals lying dead miles away. The nerves in my body formed a network of live wires, exposed, popping, near the point of conflagration. If now, with all my hopes, now when the moment to act announced itself like a giant bell tolling over the land, if now this partner who'd freely entered into a pact with me betrayed me, I knew not what heights my fury would reach. His flesh would rip, flesh as abhorrent to me in that moment as it had been enthralling for the past year. How could I bear to let him live? Impossible. And he knew it. He knew it but spoke still.

V

Yet couldn't he have been under the old woman's spell, as he'd been that night in the woods? Perhaps she, not he, spoke. Perhaps she was in league with Luke's spirit. Damn them both. Cowards of seduction.

When Michael met me in the shadows outside the crypt the following night, I already knew his position, even without reading his thoughts. Erect, determined, silent, he approached. He did not play up the pain he felt. All the same, I despised him as he uttered the words I expected to hear.

"I can't do it, Victor," he said solemnly. "I can't."

"Damn you!" I pinned him to the wall. "It was a test, sleeping in the tomb. You refused to trust me. I'll kill you, I swear."

"I'm not stopping you."

"Stop me!" I gripped his throat and would have broken his neck, but footsteps sounded on the stairs. I covered his mouth and pulled him behind a column. The intruder stopped, then retreated. I slammed Michael against the wall.

"So you want to ruin my plans, my happiness! When I can almost taste it, like blood?" My chest heaved with fury. "You like power, do you? You like to experiment with the forces of darkness?"

"No, Victor. I love you." His face was still red from the pressure of my hands on his throat.

I backhanded him. The sting brought tears to his eyes. "Traitor. I'll kill you here and now. No, wait. I'll have some amusement first. You want power? I'll show you power."

Gripping him by the arm, I took him outside and rose into the night while he clung to me. We lighted near a corner grocery store in Knoxville, just as the owner was locking the doors. I knocked on the glass, clutching Michael still. When the owner mouthed the word "closed," I shoved open the door.

"Hey, Mister, I said I'm closed." The man was 70 or so, with a widow's peak and a bulbous nose sprouting black hairs.

V

"So you are." I advanced a step, my fangs now protruding, and he ran to the counter. Before he could grab his gun, my arm was around his neck like a vise. "Behold power, Michael."

"Let him go, Victor, for God's sake." Michael pounded on the counter.

"For whose sake?" I grabbed a shock of gray hair, pulled the man's head back, and pierced his throat. Then I sucked slowly, so he would struggle a long while under Michael's gaze.

Michael came around the table and tried to tear the man away from me.

With one thrust, I hurled him into a shelf loaded with wine. Bottles crashed to the floor, staining the white linoleum as red as the blood I drank. As soon as he stood up, I bared my dripping fangs at him.

"Nature is nature," I said. "Here, try it." I reached for his arm and pulled his lips to the old man's throat.

He strained against my grip to move his face, now smeared with blood, away from the man's neck.

The old man, his eyes stretched wide in terror, groaned and struggled to breathe. Blood had drained down the collar of his shirt and collected around his pocket protector full of pens. Holding Michael with one hand and my victim with the other, I lunged at the old man's throat, sucking greedily until he collapsed behind the counter. Michael darted toward the door, but I intercepted him.

"I could use your help now." I slammed him into shelf after shelf of canned goods and cereals and laundry soap until the quaint market was as devastated as an earthquake would have left it. Then, pulling him to his feet, I licked the blood from a gash in his forehead. "The night's just begun."

Waiting inside the store until a patrol car sped down the street, I dragged Michael, bruised and limping, across an alley

V

into a large Victorian home, now shabby and divided into apartments. The unlocked back door opened onto a long, poorly lit hallway flanked by several doors. The scent was strongest from an apartment at the front of the building.

"Don't do this, Victor. Just kill me now." His dark eyes were filled with scorn.

"You're asking me for mercy?" I laughed. "No, come with me, my beloved."

The flimsy door gave way with a firm shove. A small dog scampered to the entrance and yapped hysterically.

"What's wrong, Nipper?" A woman called from down the hall. "Come see Mommy."

When the dog continued to bark, I scooped him up by the throat, strangled him with one hand, and flung him on the rug. Michael looked away.

"Nipper? Whatsa matter, girl? Come see me."

Submissive under my grip, Michael accompanied me down the hallway to the steamy room at the end. By the time the woman heard us, it was too late to run. Young and shapely, she stood in an old-fashioned tub with claw feet, reaching for a towel. She screamed at the sight of us. I jerked the towel away from her and stuffed it into her mouth. Wrapping her in one arm and Michael in the other, I carried them both into a room with a canopy bed. Like those of a mad dog, my teeth tore at her throat, her naked breasts, until blood gushed from the wounds and she lost consciousness. When Michael vomited, I shoved him to the floor and dropped her on the bed.

"What do you think—should I let her bleed to death?"

"Feed on her, damn you!" He lay on his side, deathly pale. "Put her out of her misery, for chrissake."

"Not yet." I picked up her body and laid it next to him.

"She would have been a fine catch for someone, don't you

V

think?" I got down on my haunches and stroked her chestnut hair. Her blood trailed down the uneven oak floor toward Michael and he tried to get away from it but I held him down until the blood saturated his shirt and he vomited again.

"So, you like to play with evil forces? But you didn't bargain for this, did you."

"Kill me, Victor." As he looked up his eyes started to roll back and he collapsed in his own vomit.

"No! I'm not through with you yet." I carried him to the bathroom and dunked his head in the tub until he came to. Then I dragged him to his feet and back to the bedroom for my finale. I gulped the blood spurting from the woman's throat and breasts and lapped up the floor. My lips now dripping, I kissed Michael, thrusting my tongue down his throat until he gagged and vomited once again.

"Damn you." Michael was exhausted and ill. I nearly had to carry him to the house next door toward the scent of more blood.

Just as I tried the door a police car stopped in the alley. An officer got out and shouted for us to raise our hands. In the time it takes me to break a neck, I rose, my arm wrapped around Michael. The officer fired several shots. I winced when one struck my shoulder blade, but continued on. By the time I cleared the treetops, I felt blood oozing from Michael's stomach.

"You've been hit!" I shouted against the force of the wind.

Grimacing in pain, he did not respond.

I landed with my burden in the forest clearing, laid him on the ground, and stripped off his soaked shirt to inspect the wound. The bullet had plunged deep into his bowels. With every beat of his heart, blood spurted. Blood which, linked as it was with jeopardy to his existence, gave me no delight. Wadding his shirt into a tourniquet, I pressed it against his stomach. His rib cage heaved as he struggled for breath. His skin was as hot as summer pavement.

V

"Michael, don't slip away. Fight this." I shook his shoulders gently until he opened his eyes. "There's still time. You can still drink." Holding the tourniquet in place, I stripped off my shirt and positioned my nipple near his mouth. "Drink, damn it!"

He shook his head, slowly but deliberately.

"Why? Why let yourself die when you can suck life from me? Power, eternity. Eternity with me, damn you." I brought his lips to my chest, but he would not suck.

I leaned down and spoke directly into his ear as he fought for consciousness. "This god that draws you, doesn't he command you to love? Isn't that what the Gospels teach? Then do this for love. I need you, do you hear me?"

He labored more and more to take in air as he struggled to speak. "I love you, Victor."

"Then come with me!" I whispered the words forcefully into his ear.

Desperate ideas to save him flashed through my mind—whisking him away to an emergency room, retrieving bandages to bind him, tearing out the bullet with my own hand. But only moments remained for him.

"What is this heaven you have seen—that you'd sacrifice eternal freedom for? Freedom and me. What can it offer that I can't? Tell me! If it's worth eternity, I'll follow you, by God!"

Michael turned his head. He worked to focus his listless eyes on me, as though he wanted to speak. He inhaled and released a shaky breath. He did not inhale again. His gaze froze on me.

"No!" I knelt over him and shook him violently. "No, damn you. You can't leave me alone. I'm through with the night. I want my reward." Hot tears ran from my eyes. I lifted his face and kissed his lips.

"Are you satisfied, Joshu?" I called into the night sky, whose dazzling stars seemed to mock me. "What else do you want from

V

me? Another two millennia of torture, is that it? You won't have it. I swear you won't!"

Casting a last look on the eyes no longer mysterious and penetrating, I got up and sprinted into the woods, bounding over fallen trees, snapping branches, splashing through the brook, until I reached the ledge where Michael had shown me the sun after 2,000 years of darkness. I howled like a wild animal, howled until I thought I would explode in anger. The sound resonated in the valley below and was answered by the cries of wolves deep in the thicket.

Then I tore at my hair, and clawed my face until it bled. I rolled on the rocky ground and beat it until my fists were crimson with blood. I longed to kill now, but the night was far gone and the streets of Knoxville were infested with police. So I remained brooding on the ledge until just before dawn, when I fled back to the shelter of my tomb—the tomb where only a day before Michael had slept with me.

Thirty-two

My sleep was fitful that day. Several times I awoke to Michael's voice and called out to him. In dreams I reenacted the killings I'd staged for him while he pleaded with me to stop. The old store-owner's face reddened as my arm tightened around his throat. The woman's white breasts spewed blood.

Late in the day voices awakened me, first distant but gradually louder until the speakers stood outside my grave.

"Here's where the blood stops." Andrews spoke. "Shit. He's in there."

I heard the sound of guns whisked from holsters.

"Don't kill him." Brother Matthew cried from a distance. "How can we be sure?"

V

"Get back up to your office, Brother. We'll handle this."

The abbot's footsteps grew more faint as he retreated from the crypt.

"All right, Brother Victor," Andrews shouted toward the mausoleum, "come out with your hands up, nice and slow."

For a moment I considered surrendering. When they took me up into the sunlight, I would disintegrate instantly. No more wandering, hiding, feeding. No more searching for a companion to make eternity worthwhile. But the temptation evaporated as suddenly as it had formed.

"You win, Andrews," I called. "Here I come."

I kicked open the iron gate. Facing me under the dim lights were Andrews and three other agents, all pointing revolvers at me. I approached one of the agents, a neophyte with smooth cheeks.

He backed up. "Don't take another step!"

When I did, he fired. Stunned only momentarily, I grabbed the gun from his hand and crashed it against his skull. As they fired on me, I slammed the other two agents against the wall.

Andrews hit me several times while I handled the two, but I only flinched and the wounds closed immediately.

"You finally got what you wanted, Andrews." I faced him, smiling. "The serial killer. The vampire of Knoxville. Big accomplishment for you."

Andrews continued pointing his gun at me, but he looked worried. Sweat beaded on his forehead. "Reinforcements are on the way," he said as I stepped toward him.

"Too bad for them."

I took another step and he fired.

I didn't wince. "How many more bullets? One?" I couldn't resist laughing.

"What kind of a monster are you?" He backed away toward the open mausoleum. Now his gun trembled.

V

"Let me show you." After he fired his final bullet, I grabbed the weapon from him and tossed it on the stone floor. He tried to run, but I clutched him by the neck, flinging him to the floor. Straddling him, I pinned back his arms and lowered my face until our eyes were inches away. His were full of terror.

"Don't kill me. Please. I've got a family."

"That's a pity." I nuzzled his throat for a moment and then plunged my fangs into his jugular vein. He struggled against me longer than any of my prey ever had. Even his blood seemed to resist the force of my lips, barely trickling from his throat. But when he eventually succumbed, the blood gushed into my mouth, as robust as fine wine.

Since the other agents were still breathing, I snapped their necks. Then I waited in the dank crypt until the sun set, itching to leave, energized by Andrews' blood.

When I finally opened the door to the foyer, all was quiet, the abbot nowhere to be seen. Like a submissive lamb, he'd followed orders perfectly. He must not have heard the gunshots through the thick stone walls of the monastery. I stood outside his office door and heard him explaining everything to Brother George, who responded in gravelly monosyllables. When I opened the door, they looked up, stunned.

"Brother Victor." The abbot stood behind his desk. The blood drained from his face. He glanced at Brother George, who sat in an armchair with his legs crossed, smoking as usual.

"Mr. Andrews sent me up. He asked me to give you something."

Brother Matthew stared in horror as I approached his desk. My clothes were covered with blood and my fury, no doubt, fired my glance. Brother Matthew backed away from me toward the window. Brother George put out his cigarette and got up to rescue him.

"Now, Victor," Brother George said in his gravelly voice. "They're on to you. There's no escape. If this is a mental illness—"

V

The moment he touched my sleeve, I grabbed his throat, my eyes still searing into the abbot's, and squeezed the breath out of him while he thrashed about. When I released him he slumped to the floor.

"Oh God, God." The abbot frantically surveyed the room for a means to escape. Beads of sweat formed on his pink scalp. "Please, please, Victor. In the name of God," he said as I moved around the desk.

I pressed him against the window, both hands on what little neck emerged from his habit. He pounded my chest as I strangled him until his eyes rolled back in his head.

"So much for the power of your damned god!"

Rather than satisfying me, the killings only fueled my desire to strike out against the god who stole from me the only two creatures I had ever loved. I stormed to the recreation room, where the handful of monks who were not away at universities gathered for the social hour. Four old monks watched the blaring television in a corner of the large room. Two monks played pool, while another looked on from the bar. Not a single head turned when I entered; evidently they knew nothing about my crimes or the FBI's chase.

"Like a drink, Victor?" the scrawny bald monk at the bar said. Then he noticed my bloody clothes and his mouth gaped. In an instant I grasped him by the throat and snapped his spine.

The brothers playing pool had been too absorbed in their game to notice anything. While one, short and olive-skinned, leaned over the table to make a shot, I pounded his head against it with such force that he was dead in an instant. Dazed, his curly-headed opponent tried to fend me off with his pool cue. I snatched it from him, knocked him down, and punctured his heart with it. Blood rushed from his black robe like a geyser.

The monks near the television stared at me in horror, frozen

V

in their chairs. Silver-haired Brother Augustine stood and, gathering his courage, reasoned with me, his frightened eyes darting to the bodies on the floor as he spoke. The other three rose. Two edged toward the door. I grabbed them by the throat and strangled them. When Augustine came at me I did the same to him, before turning to the last monk, the obese cook. His face pale, he backed away, clutching his chest as though his heart was failing. His eyes widened as I squeezed his throat, and he tore at my hands until I crushed his windpipe and he went limp.

I was met at the door by a new young monk, Brother Stephen, who saw the carnage and tried to flee.

"You don't think you can get away, do you?"

His terrified blue eyes looked past me at the door. Barely 20, he'd grown a soft reddish moustache after the monks teased him about his youth.

I brushed it with my fingers. Then I tore off his habit and flung his naked body to the floor.

"Oh God. Let me go, Brother Victor. Don't do this."

But without mercy, I rammed my cock into him, while he screamed in pain. When I was through, I bit into his tender throat and guzzled his blood, sweet as honey.

Maddened by a rage that had only gained momentum with the massacre, I rushed to the chapel, leaped onto the high altar and flung statues from their niches. When piles of plaster lay on the floor, fine white dust sifting down, painted hands and heads scattered over the marble, I wrenched out the tabernacle itself and hurled it into the sanctuary. The bronze doors flew open and released the ciborium, which spilled its store of wafers.

Like a wild ape, I scrambled up the reredos, tore off the crucifix that had taken possession of Michael, and hurled it across the chapel. In that moment, the room shook as though the crash had caused an earthquake. I dropped to the floor and searched the

V

darkness, struggling to keep my balance in the trembling room.

I sensed a presence. "Who is it?" I shouted. "Who is it?" The corpus from the crucifix moved, becoming supple, taking on the color of flesh.

"Joshu! So now you come to me. To hell with you!"

"It's not too late, Victor." The man who rose before me, though radiating an eerie, unnatural light, was the Joshu I had known from life. Wrapped in the loincloth he wore at his execution, blood streaming from the thorns digging into his scalp, he stood before me in all his strength and beauty. "Heaven is not beyond you. I am not beyond you."

"So you haunt me?" I blurted. "You torture souls to bring them to salvation?"

"There's still hope, Victor."

"To hell with you, Joshu. You're a traitor!"

He looked at me as he had once looked at me, not in piety, not in pity, but in devotion, attachment. Then he turned and started back to the cross.

"Joshu, no!"

I ran to him, but my hands passed through his form, as though he were vapor. He mounted the cross and solidified once more into the immobile figure who embodied a sentimental artist's conception of him.

He had jabbed my heart again. He had betrayed me with full knowledge. How many times would we repeat this scene? I would never accept his conditions. To show him, to rebel against his god...that vow I renewed then and there.

IX
Night Again

Epilogue

My view of the above-ground tombs was partially obstructed by the tall magnolia in the front yard of the mansion. But through the second-story window I could discern a row of the white mausoleums across the street, protruding like teeth from a black mouth. A crowd near the iron cemetery gates gathered around a bearded tour guide dressed in a turtleneck and jeans, who gestured toward the cemetery. I knew he was giving the speech he gave every night at the same hour. The day after my arrival in New Orleans I'd gone down to listen, hearing him explain the process of "falling through," whereby the decaying body, baked to ashes in the brick grave—in which the internal temperature often exceeded 200 degrees from the intense southern sun—

V

gradually sifted through the stacked racks to the bottom of the grave, where it mingled with the dust of its ancestors. The skull and any bones still intact on the top shelf were swept to the floor when it came time to bury the next corpse. "Falling through" was the passage to an eternal family reunion of sorts.

I had risen an hour before from the mausoleum I had claimed in the cemetery, one belonging to a family whose line had died out, indicated by the last burial date (1935) engraved in the white door. No one would disturb my slumbers in that resting place in New Orleans's Garden District. But the hot chamber had made my sleep fitful, haunted by nightmares of Michael. Upon waking, rather than crossing to the antebellum mansion I'd purchased, I often strolled the streets of the District, brooding as I passed the grand porticos, the cypresses and oaks of other old estates.

Only a week had passed since my flight from the monastery, and I continued to replay in my mind the final scenes there— Michael's death, the massacre of monks, the demolition of the chapel's sanctuary. And of course, the apparition of Joshu, pale and bleeding, once again ready to comfort and to torture my soul.

Excited by his appearance, infuriated by the promise of renewed torment, I set out to conclude the ravage I had begun. With gasoline from the storeroom, I doused the volumes in the library and trailed a stream along the wooden floors throughout the buildings. Then I set the monastery ablaze. From the grounds I watched the flames shoot from exploding windows and lick the roof. Before long, the old rafters and supports burned and the structures, one by one, collapsed. The inferno heated the grounds like a desert sun.

Then, once more, I fled to a new grave, new nights, knowing not what cloister I would next find myself in, or even if I would seek another. But I swore to myself I would not abandon a

V

predator's life until a companion promised me his eternity.

Having had enough of morbid ruminating, I wandered downstairs, out to the street, past the crowd touring the cemetery, and took the streetcar to the French Quarter. Although it was still early, Bourbon Street already reeked of piss and beer. Sleazy barkers beckoned to prospective customers outside the strip clubs. Dixieland and blues blared through open doors of restaurants and bars.

To escape the growing crowd and neon lights, I turned down a dark side street. A row of renovated shotgun houses with colorful shutters gave way to shabby brick buildings whose galleries cast shadows over the cracked, garbage-lined walks. The smell of the river rode on a breeze through the Quarter's maze of brick and wrought iron.

"Got a light?" A shirtless boy in low-waisted jeans stepped out of a doorway. His bleached hair fell to his shoulders. His smooth face, his lustrous, innocent eyes belied his profession.

I lit his cigarette. Then I took him around the corner, far from the nearest streetlight.